Copyright © 2026 MariaLisa deMora

Edited by Hot Tree Editing

All rights reserved. This book or any portion thereof may not be reproduced or used in any manner whatsoever without the express written permission of the publisher except for the use of brief quotations in a book review. This is a work of fiction. Names, characters, places and incidents are either the product of the author's imagination, or are used in a fictitious manner. Any resemblance to actual persons, living or dead, or actual events is entirely coincidental.

First Published 2026

ISBN 13: 978-1-946738-98-1

Daycare Shadows

MariaLisa deMora

DEDICATION

*My son used to pronounce "kiddie pool" as "titty pool."
Loudly. Across a hotel lobby. "MOMMA THEY HAS
A TITTY POOL!"~ Harper L. Jameson*

*Shoutout to anyone who saw friend or family struggle
with a headstrong kiddo as they grew up, and had kids of
their own anyway. Y'all brave.*

CONTENTS

ACKNOWLEDGMENTS

Well hello there. We meet again.

I don't know if I'll ever be calm about finishing a book again. After losing the muse for months upon months, and then getting my writing mojo back? Every word feels completely miraculous!

This continuation of the Sunnybrook Cottage Cozy Mysteries series was an absolute joy to write. Flowing naturally from my fingers into the computer, it held my own interest well beyond the end of the story. Which of course means there will at least be a third book. Once these characters carve out space in my imagination, they tend to live on for quite a while.

Thanks to Becky and the gals at Hot Tree Editing. Y'all make every word better. I appreciate you all more than you know.

Thanks also to the readers who took a chance on this new-to-me genre. Your reactions have fueled my soul.

Woofully yours,
~ML

Daycare Shadows

In the quiet peace of Willow Creek, Sunnybrook Cottage Daycare buzzes with giggles, crayons, and colorful dreams, until a child's shadowy sketches unveil a nightmare hidden in plain sight.

Theresa Daye-Reed cherishes her wedded bliss with charming librarian Alex, her foster daughter Emily's artistic flair, and the thriving daycare that's become a community cornerstone. But when an anonymous note begs for help deciphering a nephew's "wrong" drawings—filled with lurking shadows and eerie figures—Theresa's haven of hugs and story time spirals into a chilling enigma.

The cryptic artwork points to a web of family feuds, a forgotten estate on the town's outskirts, and whispers of a long-buried disappearance. Teaming up with Alex's research ability, Mia's street-smart insights, and even a reluctant Officer Daniels, Theresa navigates shadowy watchers, courtroom echoes, and her own budding family all while shielding her pint-sized charges from the encroaching dark.

But in a world where monsters lurk behind easels and playground slides, can Theresa illuminate the truth before the shadows swallow the light?

Daycare Shadows is a cozy mystery brimming with heartwarming small-town charm, hilarious kid quips, and spine-tingling suspense. *Wall Street Journal* and *USA Today* bestselling author MariaLisa deMora crafts a sequel where the dangers are as deep as a child's imagination, and the resolutions lead to brighter tomorrows.

Chapter One

The scent of maple syrup and fresh coffee wafted through the sun-dappled kitchen of the Maple Street house, wrapping Theresa Daye-Reed in a comforting embrace as she held a platter for Alex's deposit of the last batch of pancakes.

Alex stood at the stove, his sleeves rolled up, humming an off-key tune from one of his story-time favorites turned cartoon musical. He'd insisted on cooking again this morning, a ritual he'd started after their wedding. It was his way of grounding them before the chaos of the daycare day began. Theresa watched him with a soft smile, her wedding band catching the light as she set the table. It had been a whirlwind year since the backyard ceremony, but moments like this made it feel timeless.

The room was a testament to their budding family life, with Emily's most recent rainbow drawing stuck on the fridge, Alex's stack of library books on the counter, and a vase of wildflowers from the daycare garden Mia had insisted on sending home the day before. It was early August, the kind of morning where the Pacific Northwest sun filtered through the curtains like a promise, chasing away the night's lingering coolness.

Emily bounded into the kitchen, her dark braid swinging like a pendulum, the latest in a series of unicorn notebooks clutched under one arm. At nine, she was a whirlwind of creativity and quiet wisdom, her eyes sparkling with the idea she hadn't yet shared.

"Miss T—er, Momma T," Emily corrected herself with a giggle that made Theresa's chest ache in the best possible way, "can we do shadow puppets today? Like, with a light and everything?"

Theresa's heart did a familiar cartwheel. Hearing Emily call her "Momma T" would forever be her favorite thing of all things. It had taken months of careful fostering, therapy sessions, and quiet nights reading stories together for the title to emerge naturally, and now it felt like the most precious gift.

Theresa laughed, pulling out a chair for her. "Absolutely, witchling. We'll make sure the friendly ones win. No mean monsters allowed."

Alex turned from the stove, plating scrambled eggs with exaggerated flair. "Shadow puppets, huh? Sounds like a plan. But only if we add some library magic to it." He slid a plate in front of Emily, topped with a smiley face pancake made from blueberries and whipped cream. "Eat up, kiddo. Heroes need fuel."

Emily giggled, digging in with gusto. "Heroes like protectors? They're charged with guarding the playground so no one falls off the Exit Express." She flipped open her unicorn notebook, its pages already filled with mazes and rainbows from previous adventures. Grabbing a colored pencil from the table's centerpiece, a jar of art supplies they'd dubbed the "Emergency Inspiration Station," she started sketching quickly. "Look at this! This is a protector *shadow*. It's big and strong, but it has a heart on its chest, so everyone knows it's nice."

Alex leaned over, his eyes lighting up as he examined the drawing of a tall, willowy figure with outstretched arms, not menacing but enveloping, like a hug made of darkness turned soft. The heart was a bold red scribble, and tiny stars dotted its edges. "Whoa, Em, that's incredible. Reminds me of a book we have at the library, *Where the Wild Things Are*. You know, the monsters in there aren't really bad. They're just wild and lonely. Max tames them with a stare, but maybe your protector shadow could tame them with hugs."

Emily paused, fork halfway to her mouth, her face scrunching in thought. "Hugs? Yeah! Shadows need hugs, too, or they get grumpy like Milo before snack time. Remember when he thought the glitter was spicy and tried to eat it? Rawr, grumpy dino!"

Theresa snorted into her coffee, nearly spilling it. "Oh, I remember. Mia had to chase him around with a napkin for ten minutes. But you're right, Em, hugs fix a lot. That's a great reason for doing friendly shadows today—to show everyone that even the dark stuff can be okay if you shine a light on it."

Alex sat down across from them, his own plate piled high. He reached out his leg under the table to play footsie with Theresa, a habit that always made her smile. "Speaking of light, I found an old overhead projector in the library basement last week. It's got that vintage hum, perfect for puppet shows. I can bring it over during my lunch break if you want."

Theresa's heart warmed at the offer. This was their rhythm now: him weaving his bookish world into her daycare haven, and together creating something unbreakable for Emily. "That would be amazing. The kids will love it. And it'll tie right into Emily's idea of turning scary things into friends."

Emily beamed, closing her notebook with a satisfied snap. "I'll make protector shadows for everyone! Even for the new kids, like those twins. The way they run in circles means they need extra protection from dizziness."

The family laughed together, the sound filling the kitchen like sunlight.

Theresa glanced at the clock. It would be time to head out soon, but she lingered a moment longer, savoring the scene. This house, with its lavender walls in Emily's room and the sunroom she'd claimed as a quiet space for drafting blog posts, felt like the exit they'd all fought for in the previous year's chaos. No more apartments above the library or over the hardware store. This house was their home, with roots digging deep into Willow Creek's soil.

As they cleared the plates, Alex wrapped an arm around Theresa's waist, pulling her close for a quick kiss on the temple. "Ready for another day of glitter and giggles?"

"Always," she replied, her hand brushing Emily's braid.

Emily hopped down, grabbing her backpack. "Let's go! Shadows are waiting to be friends!"

***

Theresa balanced a rainbow-striped tote bag on one hip and the ring of keys in her other hand, the brass jangling together like a cheerful prelude as she and Emily approached the freshly repainted rainbow door of Sunnybrook Cottage Daycare.

The colors gleamed brighter than ever under the bright sun, evidence of the summer refresh she'd orchestrated with the help of Mia and Javi, Mia's brother who worked on various projects for the cottage. Even though the cottage had a grand reopening months ago, they'd petitioned Theresa to redo the paint because Mia wanted to add a few extra sparkles for luck, with bursts of glitter embedded right into the paint. Of course she'd agreed, because why not start the new term with a little extra magic?

They'd had a lovely vacation in Portland as a family, filled with bookstore visits, lazy riverside family picnics, and grown-up late-night talks about everything from favorite childhood books to the future they were building together. But finally the cottage had called them home.

It was August, and they still needed to finalize some pretty important future plans, but those conversations had been put off until they were back and grounded again in the familiar rhythm of Willow Creek.

Emily, their foster daughter turned family in every way that mattered, skipped ahead, unicorn notebook tucked under her arm like a treasure. The girl's dark braid bounced with each step, and her smile was brighter than the sun overhead.

"Momma T," Emily said in her joyful way, "don't forget we're doing shadow puppets for circle time today! No mean monsters, just friendly ones!"

"I remember, witchling," Theresa said, tugging on Emily's braid. "Let's make sure the light wins."

As she unlocked the door, a plain white envelope fluttered from where it had been placed between the door and the frame, landing at her feet like an unwelcome guest. Her name was written on the front in stark block letters, no stamp, no return address. It looked eerily similar to the anonymous note that had arrived at the end of the previous summer term, the one that had begged for help deciphering a child's "wrong" drawings. She'd set up a meeting with the child's aunt, but nothing came of it. The meeting time had come and gone, and the woman was a no-show. Theresa had set it aside as an odd occurrence, nothing more. The memory sent a tiny shiver down her spine, but she pushed it aside. Today was for fresh starts.

She slipped the envelope into her tote bag, whispering a quick version of her old prayer under her breath: "Let today be full of light, with no tears and no bites, and also nobody eating glitter. Amen."

Inside, the cottage smelled of fresh paint and the faint lemon cleaner she and Mia had used the day before. Sunlight poured through the wide windows, illuminating the low tables already set with crayons, construction paper, and jars of washable markers. The reading nook with its overstuffed beanbags waited invitingly, and the new bookshelf Alex had built over the summer held all the favorites, including *Where the Wild Things Are*, *The Day the Crayons Quit*, and a dozen others that had seen countless little hands.

Emily immediately dashed to the art corner, pulling out a fresh sheet of paper. "I want to make a welcome sign for the new kids!"

Theresa smiled, set her bag down and began working through the daycare's morning routine. She checked the fridge for snacks (all labeled, and allergen-free), tested the emergency lights (working), and flipped on the soft music that always helped ease the little ones into the day.

Within minutes, the first parents arrived. Mrs. Tennison was a new client with her three-year-old twins, who predictably and immediately began chasing each other around and around the rainbow rug, giggling as they became more and more dizzy.

There was also the young Mr. Simmon, whose four-year-old daughter clung to his leg until Theresa knelt down with a puppet who said, "Janey, I didn't see you there."

The little girl's face brightened. "I here," she responded.

"I see," the puppet said.

Janey grabbed the toy and showed it to her father, who was looking at Theresa with silent gratitude.

By midmorning, the room looked like a moderately tidy mess. Theresa and her two assistants had leaned into the perfect chaos of a daycare's new term. They encouraged many giggles, demonstrated the scratch of crayons, and solved a minor meltdown over a broken purple crayon (quickly resolved with hugs and a replacement). Now the sweet smell of apple slices ready to be passed out for snack time filled the air.

Theresa moved through it all with practiced ease, her wedding band catching the light every time she reached for a child or straightened a shelf. Alex had slipped it onto her finger during their quiet ceremony in the backyard of the cottage, surrounded by friends and wildflowers. He'd whispered, "Forever starts now," and she'd believed him.

I still believe him.

For Mia, her co-director, it was a late-arrival day, and when she breezed in around ten, her arms were full of fresh flowers from her garden. "Thought the place could use a little more color," she said, setting a vase of sunflowers on the welcome table.

Milo, her son, trailed behind her with a single flower in his hands. "I help, Miss T. I help. Rawr."

Theresa smiled at him. "You're a big help, Milo. Good job."

As the morning wore on, Theresa's mind kept drifting back to the envelope in her bag. She hadn't opened it yet. Part of her wanted to pretend it didn't exist, that the new term would be nothing but sunshine and finger paints. But the weight of it tugged at her, a reminder that Willow Creek had its secrets, even in the brightest corners.

During naptime, when the room slowly quieted to soft breathing and the hum of the white noise machine, Theresa finally pulled the note out. The paper was ordinary, the handwriting precise.

"Please help. My nephew's drawings are still wrong. There are too many shadows. I don't know who else to ask. Can we meet for coffee tomorrow?"

No salutation or signature—the note was just that plea, followed by a phone number. She compared it to the contact in her phone from last year, finding it was the same. Theresa folded the note carefully, her pulse quickening. She thought of the previous mystery she'd had a hand in, the one that had led to the unraveling of deadly town secrets.

I'd do it all over again, as long as it brought me Alex and Emily.

She tucked the note away, determined not to let it cast a pall over the day.

When the children woke, she led them in shadow puppet practice. Emily's idea, of course. Using the overhead projector Alex had dropped off, they made bunnies, birds, and dragons dance across the wall, laughing as the "monsters" turned silly and friendly under the light.

By pickup time, Theresa's arms were full of hugs, and her heart was full of gratitude. The daycare was her haven, and her calling.

Whatever the note meant, she'd face it tomorrow.

As she locked up for the night, Emily chattered about her new friends, and Theresa felt the familiar warmth settle in. Home waited with Alex, dinner, stories, and the quiet joy of building a family.

But in the back of her mind, the envelope waited too.

***

"I think you should reach out again. I remember us talking about the note from last year. Maybe something critical came up and she couldn't make it. I think if the child is still having issues, then neither you nor I would want that to continue. Especially if we can help."

Alex pressed against her foot with his. They'd taken seats on opposite sides of the couch, because Theresa liked seeing him as they talked. And Alex would never turn down an opportunity to play footsies.

"You're right, of course." She glanced at the clock on the wall. "It's almost time to turn out the light for our little witchling."

Their house on Maple Street was perfect for the family they had now. Emily loved her bedroom, walls painted in a soft lavender color, with yellow curtains as contrast. Theresa had enjoyed their time picking out paint and fabric.

"I think we need to ease her into turning off the light herself. What if we got her a different bedside lamp? Maybe one that would go on and off with a touch." He pressed both his feet against hers, rubbing gently with his toes. "Maybe one that uses claps to turn on and off."

"I'll ask Mia tomorrow. I know she's done something with Milo recently. I think she found a lamp at the hardware store with the touch thing. I'll ask her."

"Sorted," he said cheerfully. "And when will you text the shadow lady?"

"Same answer, Mr. Reed."

"Sorted again."

***

The next morning, Theresa texted the number: *Coffee, Maple Café, Saturday 10 a.m. work?*

Almost immediately she received confirmation.

Theresa wasn't sure if she was pleased or disappointed that they'd gotten back to her so quickly. That spoke to a greater need than she'd expected.

Nothing to do now but wait for the weekend.

On Saturday, after a full week of work at the daycare, she arrived at Maple Café ten minutes early, nerves humming beneath her calm exterior. The café smelled of fresh-ground coffee and cinnamon scones, a comforting contrast to the unease curling in her stomach. She ordered the café's signature lavender latte and claimed a corner table near the window, where sunlight streamed in and the chatter of other patrons provided a soft buffer.

She recognized Elena Vargas the moment the woman stepped inside. Elena was on a list of people Theresa had made earlier in the week to call about their future endeavors. She was a local business consultant in her mid-thirties, dark hair pulled into a neat bun. Her eyes scanned the room with quiet intensity. She carried a large sketchbook under one arm and held the hand of a small boy by her side. The child, who looked about five, had the same serious expression as Elena, his gaze darting curiously around the café.

"Theresa?" Elena asked, voice soft but steady.

"That's me. Good morning, Elena." Theresa stood, offering a warm smile. "You must have sent the note. And this is...?"

"Leon. Leon Latham. My nephew," Elena said, guiding the boy forward. "Say hello, kiddo."

Leon gave a small wave, then immediately buried his face in Elena's side.

They settled at the table, Elena ordering tea for herself and hot chocolate for Leon. Once the drinks arrived, Elena opened the sketchbook with careful fingers.

"First, I want to start with an apology," she began. "Right after I sent you the first request for a meeting, we had a tragedy in the family, and the meeting was overlooked. And second, I didn't know where else to turn. Leon's parents—my sister Melanie and her husband Ronald—are...they're gone. There was a plane crash as they were coming home from a retreat. That's why I get to have Leon with me. But these drawings of his..." She slid the book toward Theresa. "They're not like the usual stuff kids draw."

"Don't even think about the missed meeting. I'm so sorry you've had to deal with such a heartbreak."

Theresa opened to the first page. The drawing was surprisingly detailed for a young child. He'd drawn a house with many windows, each room filled with figures, some stick people, some more abstract. But what caught her breath were the shadows. They weren't simple outlines. They pooled in corners, stretched across floors like fingers, and in every room, darker shapes lurked just beyond the light, drawn disturbingly tall, indistinct, with a sense of watching.

She flipped pages. More houses that all looked similar, more shadows. One drawing showed a child standing alone in a room while a dark silhouette loomed behind, hand raised as if to strike. Another depicted a playground slide, but the shadow beneath it had angry eyes.

Theresa's skin prickled. "Elena, these are pretty intense."

Elena nodded, eyes glistening. "He started drawing like this after spending weekends at an estate my parents owned outside town. This was even before his mom and dad died. The place has been empty for so many years, and Melanie and Ronald were refurbishing a few things so we could put it on the market. My sister had insisted everything was fine, but Leon first came back quiet, then withdrawn. I put it down to Melanie and Ronald arguing about selling the estate. She and I were on the same page, but not her husband. He wanted to try and live out there. But then these drawings started."

Theresa studied the images again, searching for patterns. The house looked familiar. Too familiar. It was the old Whitaker place on the town's outskirts, abandoned since a shocking disappearance decades ago. She knew whispers of it had floated around Willow Creek for years.

"Has he said anything about them?" Theresa asked gently.

"Not much, have you, little guy?"

Leon shook his head, leaning against Elena's side.

"He just says 'the shadows follow.' And last week…" Elena hesitated. "He woke up screaming, saying someone was watching him sleep."

Theresa glanced out the window and froze. Across the street, half hidden behind a parked van, stood a figure in a dark coat. Tall, motionless, face obscured. Watching the café.

Her heart thudded. She blinked, and the figure was gone.

"Did you see that?" she whispered.

Elena followed her gaze. "See what?"

"Nothing. Probably just my imagination." But the unease lingered, like electricity had found a home under her skin.

They talked longer, with Theresa asking about Leon's current school experience, his parents' reluctance to seek help for him before their deaths, and Elena's fierce determination to protect her nephew. Theresa promised to think on it, maybe consult Alex for research.

"Elena, you were on a list for me to call today." Theresa laughed softly. "Alex and I are potentially looking to open a new business in town."

Elena's head popped up, and she smiled wide. "No way! I'd love to work with you to find what you need. Can you share the type of business?"

"Sure. We're considering opening a bookstore. We'd need a location that's affordable but still downtown. Everything is just discussion so far, but I'm feeling really positive that this is something we'll move forward with."

"So, it's the two of you? Would you close the daycare?"

"Us and Emily, yes. Officially, we're her foster family, but we're on a foster-to-adopt path. And no, I don't think I'd want to close the daycare. I can't imagine Alex being okay with that. We're both sort of 'get it done' people, though, so I feel good about the idea."

"I have a couple of places in mind already. Do you want to drop me an email with a day and time that works for an appointment, and any specific needs you guys have already decided on?"

"I can do that." Theresa gave her a bright grin. "More likely you'll get an email from Alex, but we're in lockstep with what we need, so you can take it and run with it."

"Sounds good."

As they parted, Elena reached over and pressed a few pages of Leon's drawings into Theresa's hand. "Please. If you see anything…"

"I will," Theresa assured her. "And you'll hear from me or Alex about an appointment."

As she walked home, the sunshine felt thinner, the streets less friendly. The shadowy watcher had vanished, but the memory remained.

***

That evening, after running an errand, Theresa arrived home to the scent of garlic and herbs and grinned. She loved Alex's famous pasta sauce. Emily was at the table, coloring a new picture of a bright sun, a two-story house, and one friendly child with dark hair and a smile.

"Look, Momma T! A happy drawing!"

Theresa kissed the top of her head. "It's beautiful, witchling."

Alex emerged from the kitchen, apron tied around his waist, glasses slightly fogged from steam. He kissed Theresa hello, lingering. "Good day?"

"Interesting," she said, and once Emily was settled with her coloring, Theresa showed him the note and drawings.

Alex's expression grew serious as he pored over them. "That house...it's the old Whitaker estate. I remember reading about it years ago. Something happened." He cocked his head to one side. "A disappearance maybe. I think it was a young woman, who was never found. The family sold it off, but the place sat empty. My memory is foggy, though, so I'll need to refresh my knowledge."

"I looked at some images of the house on the realtor's site. The drawings match the rooms with the addition of evil shadows," Theresa said quietly. "And Elena thinks Leon's visits there were what triggered this.

Oh, I noticed that on the website it's listed as Shadowbrook Manor, not the Whitaker estate."

"I think the folks who bought it tried to rename the place. Or maybe it reverted to the original owners. That sounds right. I can look that up too." Alex pulled her close. "We'll figure it out. Together."

"Guess what Elena does for a living?"

"She's a business consultant, isn't she?"

Theresa stared at him for a long minute, watching the furrows in his brow deepen as he tried to understand what she was implying.

"Yes, she is." Theresa grinned. "And we're looking for a consultant. I told her one of us would send her an email with all the must-haves we've decided we need in a business and building."

"One of us, huh? I think I understand my assignment."

She leaned close and pressed a gentle kiss against the hinge of his jaw. "I think you do."

They ate dinner, laughed over Emily's tales of carefree Saturday adventures, and tucked her in with stories. But as the house quieted, Theresa couldn't shake the feeling of being watched.

Chapter Two

Back at Sunnybrook on Monday, Theresa tried her best to focus on the children. What normally came as easily as breathing had turned challenging. Circle time brought laughter, story time brought yawns, but her mind kept returning to Leon's drawings and that fleeting glimpse of something across the street.

After the afternoon's pickup time, Theresa pulled Mia aside before she could leave. "I met with the anonymous letter writer on Saturday. It's Elena Vargas. Her nephew's drawings are, in a word, disturbing."

Mia whistled low. "The one from the earlier note?"

"The very same. I got a second message, and this time she showed. The reason she ghosted me was because Leon's parents had been killed."

Mia made a small distressed sound, like a mouse caught up in owl talons. She lifted her hand to her mouth. "I remember that. It was a plane crash. I would never have connected that tragedy with someone missing an appointment."

Theresa nodded. "I'm the same, but I still felt bad that I didn't make that connection. Back to the note, though. She brought some of Leon's drawings. They're..." She sighed. "They're *off* is the only word that truly fits."

Theresa showed her the drawings. Mia's usual humor faded as she studied the pages.

"These aren't normal kid scribbles. That's creepy as hell."

"Exactly." Theresa glanced toward the windows. "And when we were at Maple Café, I could swear someone was watching us."

Mia's eyes narrowed. "You're sure?"

"No. But it also felt off. I'm going to come to hate that word, I think."

"What are you going to do?"

"I don't know." Theresa shrugged. "You know it's going to bother me like crazy if I can't do something."

"You'll figure out what to do. I have faith in you, T."

They finished closing in companionable silence, the kind born of long friendship. Mia hugged her tightly before leaving. "Be careful, okay? And tell Alex. He loves playing detective."

"Trust me, I've already looped him in, and he'll be involved at every step." Theresa hugged Mia back.

"Bye, Milo," she called, then laughed as the small boy whirled and came back like a racing storm to thud to a stop against her legs.

Face up, smile as bright as the sun, Milo shouted, "I almost missed you! Bye, Miss T. Love you."

"Love you, little man."

Theresa watched them leave, then locked the door and shooed Emily toward the car. "Better get a move on it. Alex will be waiting for you."

Emily and Alex had started a routine where on Mondays, when he worked until eight, Emily would spend those last couple of hours with him at the library. Theresa's heart had melted a bit when Alex proposed the arrangement. He wanted time to bond with Emily one-on-one, and she loved that.

At home alone in the house, she opened her laptop to find a new email sent by what looked like a throwaway email address. The subject was *The shadows know.*

The body was blank except for one line: "Don't look too close. They notice."

Theresa stared at the screen, pulse racing. The darkness outside the window seemed deeper, more watchful.

The light in the house flickered once, then held steady.

But to Theresa, it felt like the shadows waited.

***

The next day at Sunnybrook, the morning sun filtered through the wide windows, casting playful patterns on the rainbow rug that seemed almost mocking in their cheerfulness. Theresa moved through the routine on autopilot. She was greeting parents with smiles that felt a touch too forced, settling squabbles over the red truck with gentle redirects, but her thoughts kept drifting back to those drawings. The Whitaker estate, or Shadowbrook Manor as it was called it on the realtor site, loomed in her mind like an uninvited guest.

During free play, she found herself lingering near the art corner, watching the children scribble with abandon. Emily was deep into a masterpiece of unicorns and rainbows, her tongue poking out in concentration. Theresa knelt beside her, ruffling her curls. "That's beautiful, witchling."

"Would you like to help with the sky?" Emily held out a bright blue without looking up.

"No, but you're sweet to offer."

Theresa's eyes returned to the stack of Leon's copied drawings she'd tucked into her planner. She pulled one out discreetly, comparing the stark black lines to the vibrant chaos around her. The shadows in Leon's work weren't just absences of light. They twisted with intent, almost alive. A chill traced her spine, not from fear exactly, but from the weight of a child's unspoken story of abject terror.

Mia wandered over during a lull, wiping paint from her hands on her apron. "You look like you're solving a puzzle without all the pieces. Spill more about those drawings. I couldn't stop thinking about them last night."

Theresa spread a few on the tall counter, away from the kids' prying eyes. "See this? The house is very well detailed. The gables, turret, even the wraparound porch. It matches photos of the old Whitaker place perfectly. And these figures, Mia, they're not playing. They're lurking, reaching. Elena said Leon started this after visits there, right around when his parents were arguing about selling it before the crash."

Mia traced one elongated shape with her finger, brow furrowed. "Kid's got talent, but this is beyond five-year-old stuff. It's like he's channeling something he saw, not imagined. Remember that cold case from the '70s? The disappearance at that estate? The papers called it a runaway, but my parents always whispered about foul play. What if Leon's picking up on family vibes, maybe secrets buried deep?"

Theresa nodded slowly, a knot forming in her gut. "That's what worries me, but it's not his family, though. His grandparents bought it from the Whitakers' trust. He whispers about 'shadow people' following him home. And that crash. Alex found some articles that hinted it might not have been accidental. If there's a connection—"

A sudden boom from the block corner snapped their attention to two toddlers giggling over a toppled tower, one of their assistants already hovering in case of meltdowns. Fortunately the giggling quickly turned into full-on belly laughing.

Mia straightened with a sigh. "We should dig a bit. I'll ask Javi. He knows everyone in town by now. Old shopkeepers, realtors, and a surprisingly chatty florist, so basically he's got a connection everywhere. The works. But T, don't go lone wolf on this. Don't forget, Alex's research brain could help."

"I know." Theresa gathered the drawings, but as she did, a faint detail caught her eye in one. Hidden in the garden shadows was a small well, barely sketched but unmistakable. She recalled whispers from her own childhood, something about the Whitaker well being cursed. The knot tightened further, a quiet unease settling like dust in the sunbeams.

As the morning wore on, she kept an eye on the windows, half expecting that fleeting figure from the café to reappear. But there was nothing of note. Still, the weighty symbolism of the drawings pulled on her senses, creating a silent but nearly physical plea she couldn't ignore.

***

The next day, the midmorning chaos at Sunnybrook Cottage Daycare was in full swing, a symphony of giggles, crayon scratches, and the occasional triumphant "Ta-da!" from a child unveiling their masterpiece. The room buzzed with energy, low tables scattered with construction paper, markers, and jars of glitter that shimmered like captured stardust under the sunlight streaming through the wide windows. Theresa moved through it all like a seasoned conductor as she knelt to help Priya Delgado glue a rainbow onto her drawing.

Their two assistants—Jasmine with her angelic voice and boundless enthusiasm for all things sparkly, and the ever-reliable Sarah, who handled the toddlers with quiet efficiency—had divided the kids into groups. Jasmine, in particular, had taken charge of the glittery craft station, her early childhood education degree shining through as she sang an upbeat tune to keep the little ones engaged. "Okay, friends! Today we're making sparkle monsters! Happy ones! Dip your fingers into the glue to spread on your papers, then with your other hand sprinkle the glitter, and watch the magic happen!"

The kids dove in with glee. Milo, ever the dramatic one, slathered glue onto his paper like it was frosting, then dumped an entire jar of silver glitter over it. "Rawr! My monster eats sparkles for breakfast!" he declared, shaking the excess off with such vigor that a shimmering cloud exploded into the air.

Jasmine laughed, her eyes wide. "Whoa, Milo! That's some serious sparkle power!" But the glitter had a mind of its own, drifting like fairy dust across the room— and straight onto Landon Hargrove's meticulously organized primary-color grid. Landon froze, staring in horror as his blue dots turned speckled.

Just then, the front door chimed, and Mrs. Hargrove swept in like a storm cloud, her PTA-president radar clearly detecting the need for an unscheduled visit. She was early for pickup, but that never stopped her audits.

Spotting the glitter apocalypse, her eyes narrowed. "Theresa! What is this? Glitter? You know Landon has sensitivities to...well, chaos. His naturopath says unstructured sparkle can lead to overstimulation!"

Theresa straightened, plastering on her professional smile while inwardly groaning. "Mrs. Hargrove, it's all washable and nontoxic. We're channeling it into friendly monsters today—very therapeutic."

Mrs. Hargrove huffed, brushing imaginary specks off Landon's shoulder. "Therapeutic? It looks like a disco ball exploded. Mark my words, this will end in tears, or worse, a rash." She scooped up Landon's artwork (now unintentionally festive) and departed with her usual rustle of judgment, leaving a trail of awkward silence.

Landon hung behind her, offering a tiny smile to Theresa. "Miss T, it's only a little itchy." He ran off before his mother could turn and call for him, falling into line right behind her like all ducklings did.

Mia, who had just breezed in with her arms full of sunflowers, caught the tail end and rolled her eyes. "Whew, dodged that bullet. If she saw the sensory maze Javi's fixing out back, she'd have a conniption. He's out there now, wrestling with the rosemary bushes like they're escaped convicts. 'Mia,' he says, 'this maze is gonna be epic—kids'll get lost in smells, not shadows.' Epic, my foot. It's gonna be a lawsuit waiting to happen if someone trips over a mint leaf."

Theresa chuckled, pulling out her phone to jot a quick note for *Kid Quips*: "Glitter explosion turns monster craft into disco disaster. One kid: 'My monster eats sparkles!' Another: 'But now it's itchy magic.'" She formatted it carefully, smiling at the potential for a post titled *When Sparkles Attack*. The blog was thriving, and these moments were gold.

As the laughter resumed, Theresa drifted to the art corner where little Janey Simmon was scribbling away. The four-year-old's drawing caught her eye: a sunny playground with a big, wobbly swing, but lurking off to the side was a dark, jagged shadow with what looked like angry pink eyes. By itself it was innocent enough; she surely knew that kids drew all sorts of things. But it echoed the anonymous note about "wrong" shadows too closely.

Theresa's pulse quickened. Was this a coincidence? Or some parent's prank, testing her after last year's drama?

"Janey, sweetie, what's that by the swing?" Theresa asked gently.

Janey looked up, beaming. "Scary shadow! But it hides cookies. Nom nom!"

Theresa exhaled, the tension easing. Just a kid's imagination. Still, she filed it away, a subtle reminder that Willow Creek's secrets sometimes hid in plain sight, or in crayon scribbles.

As snack time approached, the sweet smell of apple slices cutting through the glitter haze, she pushed the thought aside. For now, the light was winning.

Chapter Three

The Maple Café hummed with the evening rush, the scent of lavender lattes mingling with fresh pastries as Theresa slid into a corner booth, teddy bear nanny cam tucked discreetly in her bag—just in case. Alex had insisted on the precaution, his librarian instincts kicking in after last night's discussion about the note. "Boundaries, T," he'd said with a kiss, "but bring backup." She was there for another meeting with Elena.

"Theresa, thank you for coming." Elena sat and slid a folder across the table, her hands trembling slightly. "He's drawn more shadows."

Theresa opened the folder to reveal a child's drawing. She saw a crayon house with windows like eyes, but every room brimmed with extra shadows, showing elongated figures lurking behind furniture, under beds, even in the garden.

"The shadows won't leave him alone, will they." Theresa shook her head. "I'm not a child psychologist, but I work with kiddos every day, and these drawings are even more disturbing than the others."

She leaned closer, heart thudding. The house in the drawing was unmistakable with its tall gables, wraparound porch, and the distinctive turret that locals in Willow Creek still whispered about. Alex had looked up what information was readily available and found out the old Whitaker estate had been abandoned for decades after a young woman vanished without a trace in the 1970s. As his memory had provided, the case had gone cold, filed away as a runaway or accident, but rumors of foul play and "something wrong with the place" persisted.

She flipped to the next page. Another drawing of the house, with the same layout, but now the shadows had more definition. They were tall, humanoid shapes with what might have been hands reaching out. In one corner, a tiny stick-figure child stood alone, surrounded by darkness that seemed to press in.

"I know you know this, but these aren't typical kid drawings," Theresa said softly. "The sense of perspective and the amount of even the tiniest of details—it's almost too precise for five."

Elena wiped at her eyes. "He was always artistic, but these started right after visiting the house for the first time. I want nothing to do with the place. I'd sell it tomorrow if I had the final say. And even though he hasn't been back out there since the accident, the shadows still plague him."

Theresa studied the figures more closely. Hidden among the shadows in one room was a faint outline, almost like a person watching from behind a curtain. She felt a chill. "Has he said anything about who or what these are?"

"Just 'the shadow people.' He says they followed him home." Elena's voice cracked. "I don't believe in ghosts, Miss T. But something's scaring my nephew, and I can't let it continue."

They talked for nearly an hour about subjects covering everything that could touch Leon. Elena told her more about his parents' bitter divorce talks over the estate, the plane crash which had been ruled accidental but had been suspicious enough to warrant a full investigation, the way Leon flinched at any shadows anywhere, but most especially in their apartment.

"I can promise you I'll keep looking for a reason or cause," Theresa assured her. "My husband is the town librarian and has access to all kinds of genealogy information, so he can look into the disappearance. I'll show him these to keep him in the loop."

As they parted, Elena pressed another piece of paper into Theresa's hand. It was a close-up copy of one shadowy figure, its "face" a blank oval, but with eyes that seemed to follow you from across the page.

Theresa walked out into the dim August evening, but the sun did little to warm her. She glanced around, half expecting to see that watcher from last Saturday. Nothing. Willow Creek was going about its day with kids riding bikes home in the twilight, just the usual.

But the drawings in her bag cast a circle of distress around Theresa that she felt like a chill wind.

***

At the cottage the next day, Theresa tried to immerse herself in the children's energy. Emily led the older kiddos in a raucous game of "freeze dance" while the toddlers painted with their fingers, turning everything, including themselves, into rainbow masterpieces. *Thank goodness for painting smocks.*

But her mind kept drifting to Shadowbrook and those drawings.

During naptime, she opened her laptop in their storage room—now Mia's office—and posted a blog entry on her *Kid Quips* site that she titled *Afternoon Musings.*

"Today's thought: Shadows are funny things. They follow us, stretch in strange ways, and sometimes look like something they're not. But what happens when a child draws shadows that don't belong? The light always wins, right? Or does it? What do we do? What *can* we do?"

She added a cropped photo of one drawing and hit Publish. Within minutes, comments started stacking up for moderation, mostly parents sharing cute kid art stories. She'd leave those to the Parent Moderation Brigade, as they called themselves. Then one stood out as different.

"Shadows have eyes too. Be careful what you shine the light on. They notice." —*AnonymousUser472*

Theresa stared at the screen, pulse quickening. *Coincidence? Or something more?*

She closed the laptop as Mia burst in with two mugs of coffee. "You look like you saw a ghost. Spill. But not the coffee, because that'd be a mess."

Theresa shook her head as she accepted a mug. "Just going over the Whitaker estate stuff again. And again."

Mia whistled. "Last night, Javi and I were talking about the drawings, and he reminded me that our grandma said it was cursed after that girl disappeared. Said the shadows there were"—she swept her hands wide, voice falling into a dramatic tone—"alive."

"Don't you start." Theresa laughed, but it came out thin.

That evening, home smelled of Alex's vegetable lasagna. Emily greeted her at the door with a glittery hug. "Momma T! I made you a crown!"

"Oh, that's fabulous. And Alex cooked again. Breakfast and dinner, wow. A gal could get used to this kind of sweet treatment." She wrapped her arms around Emily and leaned closer to Alex for a kiss. "Thank you both."

Theresa wore her crown proudly through dinner, listening to Emily's stories from daycare while stealing glances at Alex. After Emily was bathed and tucked in, ready for sleep's recharge, Theresa showed him the folder.

Alex's eyes widened as he studied the newest drawings. "I know we've said it before, but this definitely *is* the Whitaker estate. The disappearance was back in '74. Clara Whitaker, twenty-three, unmarried, vanished during a family gathering. No body, no evidence. Police called her a runaway, but her diary mentioned 'watching shadows' and detailed some pretty vicious arguments about the house."

He pulled up images of old newspaper clippings on his tablet that included a few grainy photos of the manor, tall and imposing, surrounded by well-groomed gardens.

"Hauntings?" Theresa asked.

"Just rumors, nothing documented as far as I can tell. Lights in empty windows, or figures standing at the one in the attic. Locals avoid it. The family let it fall into bad shape after the scandal."

"And Elena's parents bought it in the late '80s. They never lived there. According to Elena, they bought it and left it frozen in time, with the property falling into more and more disrepair."

They sat in silence for a time, the house creaking around them like it was listening.

"Did you email Elena?" Theresa leaned against Alex's side.

"I did. I told her we need a downtown storefront and gave her a price we could justify paying. She responded with questions about shelving, electronics, warehousing." He sounded proud. "I told her everything I could remember from our conversations."

"We can use a desk in the back area as an office. Or I could share my office here with you."

He slipped his arm around her shoulders. "And what do you propose we could do in that shared office?" He pressed a kiss against the side of her head. "Anything I'd be interested in, perhaps?"

"Maybe." She smiled, the depths of her happiness seeming endless. "Maybe probably."

***

The next afternoon, Elena brought Leon to the cottage for a supervised playdate. Theresa had suggested it gently, hoping that maybe Emily's bright energy could help the boy open up.

As expected, Emily quickly took Leon under her wing, encouraging him to pick an activity. Almost immediately, the two children gravitated to the art corner. Emily, ever the welcoming soul, offered Leon her favorite unicorn crayons. "You can draw anything! Even monsters, but maybe make them friendly ones."

Leon hesitated, then began. His drawing started innocent with a house and a tree, but soon the shadows crept in, long fingers stretching across the page.

Theresa and Elena watched from nearby. Leon was cautious, hands trembling, and his tangible fear set her heart aching. Emily chatted nonstop, undeterred. "My

Momma T says shadows are just light's way of playing hide-and-seek."

Leon paused, looking up with serious eyes. Then he leaned close to Emily and whispered, so quietly that Theresa barely caught it, "The shadow people don't play. They wait. And they know your name."

Emily blinked, then smiled uncertainly. "That's silly. Shadows can't know names."

But Leon's face was pale, his small hands clutching the crayon.

Theresa left Elena's side and approached. "Hey, kiddos." She put one knee to the floor, making sure she was on their level. "That's cool, Leon. Want to tell me about your picture?"

He shook his head, eyes darting to the windows as if expecting something to appear.

Elena gathered him up, thanking Theresa with tears in her eyes. "He talked to her. That's more than he's said to me in weeks."

As they left, Theresa noticed Leon glance back at the rainbow door, then up at the sky, and finally over to where the afternoon sun cast long, reaching tree shadows across the lawn.

***

That night, after Emily was asleep, Theresa and Alex were curled up on the couch when she showed him the blog comment. He frowned. "Could be random, but...let's be careful."

They discussed next steps. Playing off their strengths, they decided Alex would dig deeper into town records, while Theresa would keep an eye out at daycare. But the unease lingered.

As Theresa checked the locks before bed, she glanced out the living room window. Across the street, under a streetlamp, a patch of shadow seemed...darker. Deeper. For a moment, it almost looked like a figure.

She blinked. Gone.

She found Alex tucking Emily into her princess bed and almost asked him to come and look with her. *So he can tell me I'm not losing my mind.* Then she quickly vetoed her own thought, because it was so unlikely on the face of things.

In bed, Alex pulled her close. "We'll protect her. Protect them all."

Theresa nodded, but sleep came slowly. In the quiet just before she dropped off, she thought she heard the faintest whisper, like a child's voice saying a name.

Her name.

Chapter Four

Sunnybrook Cottage buzzed with the familiar rhythm of morning arrivals, parents dropping off sticky-fingered charges with hurried hugs and a side dose of Mrs. Hargrove's reminders about peanut- and quinoa-free snacks.

Theresa watched as Elena navigated her way through the door, Leon clinging to her leg like a shy koala, a backpack slung over one small shoulder. They'd agreed on a two-week trial at the daycare. Theresa hoped by giving him normal kid things to focus on, they might break his obsession with menacing shadows.

"Come on in, Leon," Theresa said, crouching to his level with her warmest smile. "We've got a special art table just for you. Emily made sure it has crayons in every color of the rainbow."

Leon peeked out from behind Elena, his dark eyes wide but curious. He clutched a rolled-up paper, another drawing no doubt. As Elena signed the clipboard, Theresa caught Mia's eye from across the room, where their assistant Jasmine was already wrangling a glitter explosion. Sarah, their other assistant, was in the kitchen working on snacks. Having so much help had felt like a luxury at first, but now she couldn't imagine handling everything again with just herself and Mia.

We were younger and crazier.

"First-day jitters?" Mia mouthed.

Theresa nodded subtly. But as Leon unrolled his latest masterpiece, a playground with shadows stretching unnaturally long, like fingers reaching for stick-figure kids, she felt a chill despite the sun streaming through the rainbow door.

Theresa watched Leon settle at the small table, his fingers immediately seeking out the black crayon from the rainbow assortment. Emily hovered nearby like a gentle satellite, offering encouragement in her bright, matter-of-fact way. "You can make the shadows smile if you want," she suggested. "Mine always do when I give them hats."

Leon didn't respond, but his crayon moved in slow, deliberate strokes.

Theresa busied herself with the other children, running the gamut from helping a toddler glue feathers to a paper bird to breaking up a disagreement over a favorite yellow marker, but she kept glancing back.

Leon's drawing took shape quickly. She saw the familiar gabled roof of Shadowbrook Manor, the porch that wrapped like an embrace, and then the shadows. They weren't confined to corners anymore, though. They spilled out of the house entirely, long tendrils stretching across the lawn toward stick-figure children on swings and slides. One shadow curled around a little girl's ankle, pulling. Another reached toward a boy who looked suspiciously like Leon himself.

Mia sidled up beside Theresa during a brief lull, wiping glitter from her hands. "He's been staring at the dark corner by the bookshelf for the last ten minutes," she murmured. "Won't turn his back on it. The kid's terrified of shadows that aren't even moving."

Theresa followed Mia's gaze. Leon sat rigid, crayon paused mid-stroke, eyes fixed on the wedge of dimness where the sunlight didn't quite reach. Nothing there— just dust motes drifting lazily. But Leon's small shoulders hunched as if something stared back.

"I'll talk to him after snack," Theresa said quietly. "Gently. But I'm going to disrupt this fixation now."

She walked toward the bookshelf, pausing deliberately when she was directly between Leon and the shadows. When she looked back at him, he'd shifted his attention to the paper in front of him.

The morning passed in fits of normalcy with off-key songs, a story time filled with questions and interruptions, and outdoor play on the sunny lawn where shadows were short and harmless under the noon sun. Leon stayed close to the building, avoiding the open grass. When they returned inside for quiet time, he refused to lie on a mat near the window. "Too bright," he whispered, but his eyes flicked toward the corners again.

Theresa moved the mat to the middle of the room and knelt beside him with a soft blanket. "Want to tell me what you see over there?"

Leon clutched the blanket to his chest. "They follow. Not just here. Everywhere. They know where I go." His voice was barely audible. "They followed Mommy and Daddy too. Before the plane." He pulled in a sharp breath and gave an almost soundless "Boom" that nearly broke Theresa's heart.

She smoothed his hair, the way she did for Emily on hard days. "We're going to keep the light on, okay? All the lights we need."

But as naptime settled over the room, his unease grew. Theresa wondered if she was causing at least some portion by being someone Leon associated with shadows now.

She caught Mia's eye and nodded toward the garden door. She just needed half a minute of free breathing and sunshine on her skin, and she'd be reset and ready to help Leon handle his anxiety.

Theresa slipped partway through the door for her moment of fresh air and froze.

In the narrow strip of garden behind the cottage, where wildflowers tangled with the fence, a patch of shadow stood apart from the others. Tall. Human-shaped. Motionless. The sun slanted across the grass, but this darkness refused to shrink or shift. It seemed to lean closer to the building, directly toward the windows where the children slept.

Theresa's hand went to the shelf behind her. The teddy bear nanny cam, reactivated for the daycare that morning at Alex's insistence, sat ready. She pulled it out, aimed carefully through the glass pane of the door, and pressed Record. The figure didn't move. Didn't flicker. Just watched.

Heart hammering fast and hard, she held the camera steady for a full minute. When she finally lowered it, the shadow had vanished. Dissolved into ordinary light and leaf patterns as if it had never been.

Theresa immediately went to where the shadow had been and found shoe-shaped impressions in the loose dirt. Then a gust of wind swirled across the dirt, rapidly wiping away the proof that someone had been right there.

Back inside, she reviewed the footage on her phone in the office while Mia watched the room. It was a little grainy, but the tall silhouette showed up against the garden, darker than it should have been, edges too diffuse but still unmistakable. And for one brief second, as the camera zoomed, a suggestion of a face. No features, just blank, and oval, like the copy of Leon's latest close-up drawing.

She texted Alex immediately: *Caught something on cam. It was in the garden. Same as drawings. Will you be coming home early? I can bring the camera home.*

His reply came fast: *On my way to the cottage right now. Don't go back outside alone.*

Alex was as good as his word, as he showed up at the back door just a few minutes later. His appearance at the daycare wasn't novel, because he still did reading time at least once a week under his librarian duties. But you'd never know it from the squeals of happiness that came from all the kiddos, Emily in particular. He got pulled into a debate about lined paper versus sheets with a grid pattern, because Emily wanted to know how best to scale up one of her drawings.

"No, no. See, if I assign each item a set number of grids, then I could double it on a different piece of paper and have a drawing twice as big." Emily was wide-eyed, excited. "Can I come back to the library with you? I bet there's a book on art that'll tell me what I need to know."

"Ask Momma T, but it's fine with me." He gave Emily a sideways hug. "You're such a brainiac, Em."

"Momma T, can I go back to the library with Daddy A?"

That stopped Theresa in her tracks. It was the first time Emily had assigned Alex a personal name, and she loved it. She could see from the expression on Alex's face that he loved it too.

"Sure thing, butter bean. I need Daddy A's attention for a minute right now, though. Just a minute." She turned around and gave Emily her back, waving both hands in front of her eyes, trying to dry up the instant tears.

Alex's arms folded around her as he rested his chin on her shoulder. "Daddy A," he whispered. "I don't hate it." He gave her a squeeze, and Theresa sighed.

"I don't hate it either." She waved at her eyes a final time. "I've got the nanny cam bear in the office."

"I'll grab it and Em and go back to the library. Let me know when you're headed home, yeah?"

"Will do." She giggled. "Daddy A."

***

Elena arrived for pickup looking more exhausted than ever. Leon ran to her, bringing his newest drawing like evidence. Theresa pulled Elena aside while Mia distracted the boy with a puzzle.

"He's been fixated on the corners all day," Theresa said. "And he said the shadows follow him everywhere. Even followed his parents."

Elena's face crumpled. "I didn't want to say more before. My sister, Leon's mom, she worked for a development firm called Willow Development. They've been pushing to buy up old estates like Shadowbrook and turn them into luxury condos. My brother-in-law hated the thought of selling, said he wanted to be the generation that brought the place back from ruin. He and Melanie didn't agree on what to do. Not at all. The retreat they were flying back from? It was supposed to be a last-ditch effort to save their marriage. But the crash..." She swallowed. "I've always wondered if someone wanted that property cleared of obstacles. The family secrets, the old scandal, Clara Whitaker's disappearance in '74. She would have been the last heir. She vanished the night the family was supposedly selling shares in some shady land deal. Corporate ties that go back generations."

Theresa felt the puzzle pieces in her mind shift. "So, the shadows...maybe they're tied to whatever happened there. Protecting it. Or a warning."

Elena nodded. "Or punishing anyone who tries to sell."

As Elena led Leon away, the boy turned back to Theresa. "Thank you for the light," he said solemnly.

Theresa managed a smile. "Anytime, kiddo. See you tomorrow."

***

That evening, Emily greeted her at the house door with arms full of crayons and paper. "I made something for Leon!" She thrust forward a drawing. It was of a bright yellow sun, the daycare cottage, and beside it, a single shadow—tall, humanoid, but smiling. It stood between the cottage and a smaller stick figure that looked like Leon. "It's a protector shadow," Emily explained proudly. "Like a guardian. So the mean ones can't get close."

Theresa's eyes stung with so much pride. She pulled Emily into a hug. "That's perfect, witchling. He's going to love it. You're an extraordinary girl, Em."

Later, after Emily was tucked into bed with her new "protector" taped above her pillow, Theresa and Alex huddled over the laptop in their kitchen. The nanny cam footage played on a loop as Alex cross-referenced old town records he'd pulled from the library archives. An entire section was about Clara Whitaker, last seen arguing with developers on the manor grounds. He'd found a groundskeeper's log that mentioned "unnatural shadows" gathering near the old well the night she vanished. No sign of her body was ever found. The case had been closed as "probable runaway."

Alex closed the file. "We need to go to Shadowbrook. See it ourselves. But not either of us alone. Both of us will need to go."

Theresa nodded, but her gaze drifted to the window. Outside, the streetlamp flickered. A deeper patch of darkness pooled beneath it, too solid, too still.

She reached for Alex's hand. "They're noticing us now."

He squeezed back. "Then we notice them right back."

Outside the quiet house, the shadows lengthened just a little more. Watching. Waiting.

But inside, the light held. For now.

***

The midmorning lull at Sunnybrook Cottage Daycare provided the perfect window of time to do interviews for potential clients, in that sweet spot after drop-offs but before the snack-time rush. Theresa had offered to sit in on this one, partly to support Mia as co-director, but mostly because the application had caught her eye. It was for a five-year-old boy named Orlando, whose parent-described traits—dramatic flair, endless energy, and a penchant for "roaring like a dino"—all sounded eerily like a clone of Milo. It promised to be entertaining, at least.

Mia had set up in the front of the playroom, a cozy space with low shelves of board books and a view overlooking the rainbow rug. Theresa perched on a spare chair in the corner, notebook in hand for potential *Kid Quips* gold, while Mia straightened the allergen chart on the wall.

"Ready for Mini-Milo?" Mia joked, her dark hair twisted into a bun held by a glittery crayon. "If this kid's half as chaotic, we'll have double the quips but also double the cleanup."

The door chimed, and in walked Ms. Strathern, a harried but smiling woman in her mid-thirties, clutching a tote bag overflowing with kid snacks and a stuffed tiger. Trailing behind her was Orlando, a mop of curly hair framing wide eyes that immediately began to scan the room like an explorer on safari. He was the spitting image of Milo in energy, already bouncing on his toes, the soles of his sneakers lighting up with each step.

"Welcome to Sunnybrook!" Mia greeted them warmly, shaking Ms. Strathern's hand. "I'm Mia Torres, co-director, and this is Theresa Daye-Reed, our founder. Have a seat and tell us about Orlando."

Ms. Strathern settled into the chair, pulling Orlando onto her lap, though he wriggled like a live wire. "Thanks for seeing us on short notice. I'm Sabrina, a single mom, and I work in graphic design from home. Orlando's a handful, but the best kind. He's five, loves dinosaurs and anything that roars. We're new to Willow Creek. We moved for a fresh start after...well, family stuff."

Theresa nodded sympathetically, jotting a note: "Fresh starts and roars—both are a Sunnybrook specialty." She caught Orlando's eye and waved. "Hi, Orlando! I'm Miss T. What's your tiger's name?"

Orlando beamed, holding up the toy. "This is Rex! He's a good tiger. He eats bad guys for breakfast. Rawr!" He made Rex "bite" the air, his roar echoing dramatically through the area.

Mia laughed, leaning forward. "A good guy, huh? We love those here. Our playground has an Exit Express swing guarded by friendly shadows drawn by our kids. Orlando, do you like drawing?"

Orlando nodded vigorously, nearly toppling off his mom's lap. "Yeah! I draw dinos and monsters. But not scary ones. Mine have hearts and eat cookies. Mommy says no glitter, though. It gets in my nose and makes me sneeze like a dragon!"

Ms. Strathern chuckled, ruffling his hair. "He's allergic to chaos but still thrives in it. His old daycare was too structured—no room for his imagination. I heard about Sunnybrook from the *Kid Quips* blog. Those stories sold me. It sounds like real kids having real fun."

Theresa's heart warmed; the blog's reach never ceased to amaze her. "We're all about nurturing that spark. Mia, why don't you walk them through our day?"

Mia dove in with practiced ease, outlining the open floor plan, circle time with songs (Jasmine's specialty), the sensory garden for tactile play, and the nap room with glow-in-the-dark stars. "We emphasize safety and creativity. We do have nanny cams if needed, but we run mostly on trust and hugs. Any allergies to worry about? We've got protocols tighter than the lunch lady's snack audits."

As Mia spoke, Orlando slipped off his mom's lap and wandered to the edge of the carpet, peering at the playroom where a few lingering kids chased bubbles. "Mommy, look! Rainbow door! Is it magic?"

"It sure feels like it," Theresa said, joining him. "It leads to adventures. Want to see the art corner? You can draw a dino while we chat."

Orlando's eyes lit up. "Yes! With sparkles?"

Mia exchanged a glance with Theresa. They both knew that sparkles meant glitter, and glitter meant potential sneeze-fest. "How about markers first? We can hold off on the glitter until later. Much later."

In the playroom, Orlando plopped down at a low table, grabbing crayons with gusto. His drawing emerged quickly as a T-Rex with a heart on its chest, munching cookies under a rainbow. "See? Not scary, but strong!"

Milo, spotting the newcomer from across the room, trotted over. "Dino! Mine too! Rawr!" He shook his stuffed dino at Orlando, and the two boys instantly bonded, their roars harmonizing in a chorus that had the assistants grinning. "I'm Milo."

"I'm Lando," Orlando shrilled. "We're both O's!"

"Yes, you are. Two birds of a feather. The O's boys." Theresa smiled at the boys, feeling as if she was watching the beginning of a grand friendship.

Back in the office, Ms. Strathern signed the forms with a relieved sigh. "He fits right in. When can he start?"

"How about Friday?" Mia suggested. "That'll give him one day to be hyper with all the new, and then a regular weekend. By Monday he'll be all settled in."

As they wrapped up, Theresa jotted one last quip: "New kid's dino: 'Eats bad guys for breakfast—and maybe shadows? Rawr!' Milo's twin in sparkle-spirit?" It would make a perfect blog teaser.

Walking them out, Theresa felt a quiet satisfaction. Another family finding their exit to light, even amid the shadows still lurking in her own mystery. But for now, the roars of play chased them away.

Chapter Five

The art corner of Sunnybrook Cottage had transformed into a fortress of creativity, low tables piled with paper, markers, and the ever-present jar of googly eyes. Theresa drifted over, pretending to review the stock of markers, her eyes on Leon as he hunched over a fresh sheet, black crayon scratching furiously.

Emily sidled up beside him, her own notebook open. "Whatcha drawing, Leon? Can I add a rainbow?"

Leon paused, crayon hovering. "Shadows don't like rainbows. They hide in them." His whisper was barely audible, but it lodged in Theresa's chest like a splinter.

She crouched, keeping her voice light. "Shadows are just light's friends playing tag, sweetie. Want to tell me about yours?"

But Leon shook his head, adding another layer of black to the page. It looked like a bedroom with shadows crowding the bed like uninvited guests.

***

By midmorning, Leon's behavior had shifted from quiet fixation to outright evasion. During free play, he refused to join the group on the rainbow rug for songs, instead paradoxically slipping behind the bookshelf where the deepest corner met the wall. The darkest shadow in the cottage. Theresa found him curled there, knees to chest, eyes fixed on the thin line of shadow creeping along the baseboard as sunlight shifted through the window.

"Leon? It's okay to come out when you're ready," she said softly.

He shook his head violently. "They're playing the shadow game. If I move, they win. They hide and wait, and then they grab." His small hands clenched into fists. "They grabbed Mommy and Daddy. In the sky."

Theresa's breath caught. She sat on the floor beside him, not touching, just present. "The shadow game sounds scary. Can you show me how it works? Maybe we can change the rules."

He didn't answer, but when Emily peeked around the shelf with a puppet dragon, Leon allowed her to sit nearby. Emily made the dragon "breathe" light from a flashlight, turning the dark corner golden. For a moment, Leon's shoulders relaxed. Then he whispered, "They don't like light. That's why they come back stronger at night."

***

That afternoon, Theresa called Dr. Macy, the child therapist who'd helped Emily through her early foster days. After closing the daycare and then dropping Emily at the library with Alex, she met the good doctor at the Maple Café, the same corner table where Theresa had first seen Elena and Leon. Theresa spread out the latest drawings: bedrooms swallowed by darkness, figures with elongated arms reaching from walls, a small boy hiding under covers while shadows pooled like ink around him.

One at a time, Dr. Macy studied the drawings carefully, her expression calm but grave. "These aren't typical fantasy monsters. The repetition, the way the shadows encroach on personal space, it's classic trauma expression. Children often externalize overwhelming experiences through art when words feel unsafe. The 'shadow people' could symbolize loss, fear of abandonment, or even perceived threats that feel inescapable. The plane crash and losing his parents would be traumatic enough, but if there were preexisting tensions such as arguments he overheard, instability in their day-to-day, he might be projecting those as pursuing entities."

Theresa nodded. "He's terrified of dark corners now. Hides during play. Says the shadows are playing games and winning."

"Trauma doesn't always look like flashbacks in kids this young," Dr. Macy said. "It can manifest as hypervigilance, avoidance, magical thinking. Typically, I'd recommend gentle exposure through controlled light play, and talking about feelings through puppets. But Theresa, if this escalates, he will likely need formal sessions. And you should watch carefully for signs that it's more than grief. Sometimes drawings like these hint at deeper fears, if not abuse." She paused. "You're doing the right thing by noticing."

"I hope so."

***

At home that evening, Alex had news from the library's microfiche archives and a returned call from the county records office. He spread printouts across the kitchen table while Emily colored nearby, humming.

"Shadowbrook's history is messier than we could have ever thought," Alex said. "Clara Whitaker disappeared in '74 during a family meeting about selling shares in the estate to developers. That much is known. Check this, though: It was Horizon Properties, the parent company for Willow Development, the firm Elena's sister worked for all those decades later. But the real kicker was that it was a disputed inheritance. Clara appears to have been the sole heir after her parents died young. Her uncle contested the will, claiming Clara was unstable, maybe even suicidal. But there are notes on the filings that don't make any sense. A new name in the mix, but it's not clear who they might be. Her uncle tried to take control, but she vanished before the court ruled. The estate went into trust limbo. Fast-forward to when Elena's parents bought the place. They didn't do anything with it, and the two sisters, Elena and Melanie, inherited rights when their parents passed. It's not clear if the kids knew about the property before then. Melanie and her husband, Ronald, were refurbishing to sell, but scuttlebutt says they were pressured by Willow to flip it quickly—which runs counter to Ronald wanting the property to stay in the family and become a primary residence."

Theresa's eyes widened. "That's quite the soap opera."

"It gets better. I found a bunch of family secrets buried in the probate filings from the Whitakers. I'm still digging through it all. There are all kinds of accusations of undue influence, hidden debts, even a sealed affidavit about Clara's 'watching shadows' diary entries."

Theresa stared at the grainy photo of the old manor. "So the shadows Leon draws...maybe they're echoes of that old dispute? Something supernatural protecting the place? Or is a human someone pushing the myth to force Elena to keep the property? She was clear that she wanted to sell as quickly as possible, but I don't know if they've settled all the legalities from her sister and brother-in-law dying or not. Maybe she can't sell yet?"

Alex rubbed his temples. "There's always the chance that Leon could be picking up on adult stress. Elena's grief, or guilt, and likely whatever his parents were fighting about. But the timing with the crash is suspicious."

She reached out and took his face in her hands, kissing him softly. "Well, we won't solve this tonight. Let's go to bed before you give yourself a headache."

He wrapped an arm around her shoulders, tucking her underneath his chin. "Can't have that now." She felt him press a kiss to her temple. "To bed we go."

***

The next evening, Elena called in a panic. Her apartment had been broken into while she and Leon were at the park. Nothing valuable had been taken—she said all her electronics were untouched, cash still in a kitchen drawer—but Leon's sketchbook was gone. All the drawings. Every page of shadows.

"They knew what they were looking for," Elena whispered over the phone. "The door was jimmied cleanly. No forced-entry mess. It feels professional."

Theresa's stomach dropped. She remembered the watcher at the café, and the garden figure on the nanny cam. "Elena, call the police right now and make sure you're locked up tight. Plan on bringing Leon to the cottage tomorrow. That way we can keep him close." She paused. "And let me know if you need me or Alex to come over and wait with you. We can do that if you need."

"Okay. No." Elena made an obvious attempt to calm herself. "I mean, yeah, calling the police makes sense. But we'll see you tomorrow. We're okay."

***

Leon clung to Elena's hand the next morning when she brought him during drop-off time. She dropped to a knee and whispered something to him, and he flung his arms around her neck, holding on tightly. Theresa gave them a moment before she joined them on the floor. Leon gradually let go of his aunt, twisting to look at Theresa.

"Hi, Leon." She smiled at him. "I'm so glad you're able to join us today. What do you think will be your favorite activity?"

He looked around the room, pointing wordlessly at the art corner.

"Drawing is always a fun time. Is it okay if Emily draws over here with you?"

Leon nodded, then turned and buried his face against Elena's neck.

"Sometimes it's hard to let go of the ones we love, isn't it?"

He nodded again. When he swung around to face Theresa, his face was wet with tears.

"Oh, buddy, you're having a hard morning." Theresa settled on the floor and opened her arms. "Come here. We can sit here as long as you want."

It took gentle encouragement from Elena, but eventually Leon was safely in Theresa's embrace.

"Auntie will be back for pickup. You'll be safe here, Leon." He was trembling as Elena pressed a kiss to his cheek.

Theresa said, "See you soon, Elena."

By circle time, Leon had warmed up, making fast friends with Milo, who adored Emily, so it was a naturally sorted collection of kids who sat together on the carpet, Orlando in the same group. After circle time and midday cleanup, they migrated to one of the art desks. Theresa gave them a few minutes to become engrossed in their creations before she wandered their direction.

What she found was Emily instructing the three boys on creating a protector shadow. Milo and Orlando were addressing the request with their normal abundant enthusiasm, drawing in wide swooping lines using brightly colored crayons. Emily's protector was painted in rainbow strokes, colored carefully within the lines using a bold yellow crayon.

Leon's protector was gray. And tiny. It stood between a small stick figure with dark curls and a huge, detailed black shadow with an open mouth, threatening to devour the figure.

At least it's not all in black.

Milo rawred, and she realized he'd changed his shadow into a T-Rex shadow. "Shadows are scared of my teef. Rawr. Chomp."

Officer Daniels arrived at Sunnybrook during lunchtime, notepad in hand. Theresa showed him the nanny cam footage of the tall, unmoving shadow in the garden and described the café sighting, the blog comment, and the escalating drawings. Daniels listened without interruption, then asked what she knew about the break-in.

"Not much, just what Elena said last night."

"Could all be coincidence," he said, but his tone lacked conviction. "Stolen art supplies? Used at that?

Odd target. We've filed the report, dusted for prints, and will check nearby cameras. But if this ties to the estate, it might be more than random." He glanced at Leon, who sat coloring with his little group of friends under Mia's watchful eye. "The kid's safe here?"

"Safer than anywhere," Theresa said.

***

That afternoon, Theresa posted a gentle entry on *Kid Quips*, titled *Friendly Shadows: When Darkness Needs a Hug*. She shared a cropped drawing of Emily's protector shadow smiling beside a small figure and wrote about helping children reframe fears, turning monsters into guardians. "Light always finds a way," she ended. "Even from deep within the shadows."

The post exploded. Shares, likes, comments from parents sharing sweet stories. Then the suspicious ones appeared, making her glad she'd kept the blog comments moderated. Nothing would show online, just in the admin window.

"Shadows don't hug. They take." — *AnonymousUser819*

"Be careful shining lights. They hate being seen." — *ShadowWatcher23*

"Some drawings should stay hidden. Or else." — *NoName568*

Theresa's skin prickled. She promptly moved the worst comments into a hidden folder, but the unease she felt lingered.

That night, as she locked the cottage's front door, she glanced across the street. Under the streetlamp, a figure stood cloaked in a dark coat with their face obscured. Watching her.

She blinked, and it was gone.

But the shadows felt closer now, pressing in like they knew her name.

Inside their home, Emily slept with her protector drawing taped above her bed. Leon would soon join them for a few days; Elena had asked, because there was safety in numbers.

Theresa turned to Alex, who waited for her by the door. "We can't wait anymore. We need to go to Shadowbrook. See what's really there."

He nodded, pulling her close. "Together. But we bring light. Lots of it."

Chapter Six

Shadowbrook Manor loomed at the edge of Willow Creek like the setting for a forgotten fairy tale, its Victorian turrets piercing the cloudy sky, ivy clawing up the weathered stone and reaching for the overcast sky. Theresa parked her car on the gravel drive, Alex in the passenger seat with his research folder, Emily bouncing in the back.

"Is this a castle, Momma T?" she asked, eyes wide.

"More like a mystery house," Theresa replied, stepping out to meet Elena at the grand doors. Leon peeked from behind her, waving shyly.

The invitation for a "playdate research trip" had seemed innocent enough, but as they entered the dim foyer, a chill prickled Theresa's skin. Dust motes danced in slivers of light, and the air smelled of old books and secrets.

Elena led them to the drawing room, where Leon's remaining artwork covered a table. Each piece appeared darker than the last, shadows multiplying like rabbits.

The children gravitated immediately to the wide bay window that granted a sweeping view over a wild-looking flower garden. Emily spread out her crayons and construction paper on the faded Persian rug, chattering about making "castle maps," while Leon sat cross-legged beside her, silent but watchful. Theresa and Alex exchanged glances with surreptitious nods. To Theresa, the atmosphere inside the house felt heavier than it should, as though the walls themselves were listening.

"This is the first time he's been back out here." Elena ran her hand through her hair, looking troubled. "I worried about bringing him today, but he insisted on it. Thank you for agreeing for him to stay over for a few days." She sighed heavily. "I think he needs a break from me, maybe." She shook her head. "He draws this room most frequently, and that's scary enough," she whispered. "But the basement...he simply can't bear it."

Elena gestured toward the portraits lining the stairwell wall. "The Whitaker family gallery, with all its checkered past," she said wryly. "Her great-grandparents, grandparents, parents, and Clara Whitaker herself." She pointed to a young woman in a stylish-for-the-time dress, her dark hair pinned in an elegant updo. The painted eyes appeared to follow them as they moved. To Theresa, they were too sharp, too knowing. "Leon swears they watch him. I used to laugh it off. Now? I'm not so sure."

Alex stepped closer, studying the frames. "These are original oils. Expensive for the era. And look at this one." He tilted his head while looking at Clara's likeness. "The varnish has cracked in odd patterns. Almost like something was scratched into it later. There's no design, though. I bet it could be repaired."

Theresa shivered. The floorboards creaked underfoot with every shift of weight, a slow, deliberate groan that seemed to answer their movements. She tried to focus on the children. Emily was drawing a cheerful turreted castle with rainbow flags; Leon's paper already bore the familiar gabled roof of the manor itself, but the windows were blacked out entirely, as though the house had swallowed its own light.

"Let's keep things easy," Theresa suggested. "Maybe explore the garden first? Fresh air might help." She held out her hand for Emily's. "Come on, witchling. Let's find an adventure."

They stepped outside. The garden was a tangle of roses and perennials gone wild. Theresa saw multiple stone benches, cracked and moss-covered, with a dry fountain at the center shaped like a weeping angel. Emily ran ahead, laughing as she chased a butterfly. Leon stayed close to Elena, gripping her hand until his knuckles were white.

Theresa noticed the old well near the back fence. It was boarded over, but the wood looked newer than the rest of the decay. Alex followed her gaze.

"That's where the groundskeeper's log mentioned the 'unnatural shadows' gathering the night Clara disappeared," he murmured. "Right beside the well."

A soft thud sounded from inside the house. They turned. Leon pulled away from Elena's hand and ran back to the house. Everything seemed to be happening in fast-forward, until Leon stood frozen on the threshold, staring inward toward the hallway that led deeper into the manor.

"It's there," he called back to them. "The basement. It wants to play."

Elena paled. "He's never said anything like that before."

Theresa hurried to where Leon stood and knelt. "What does it say, Leon?"

He shook his head, eyes huge. "It says, 'Come see what we kept.'"

The adults exchanged looks. Against every instinct screaming caution, they agreed to let him show them. Only as far as the doorway, though, no farther. Elena flicked on every light switch they passed. The hallway bulbs buzzed and flickered, casting jittery pools of yellow on the checkered floor tiles.

Emily hung on Alex's arm, watching her new friend carefully. "You don't have to listen to it."

"Yeah, I do." The basement door stood at the end of the corridor, heavy oak, iron hinges rusted but sturdy. Leon stopped three feet away, trembling. "It's down there," he said. "The shadow that eats."

Emily, brave as ever, tugged Theresa's sleeve. "Can we draw it first? So it's not so scary?"

They retreated to the table where the drawing supplies were. Leon accepted a fresh sheet and the blackest crayon Elena could find. His hand moved faster than Theresa had ever seen, lines slashing across the page. A tall figure, stick-straight and featureless except for a wide, white oval, bent over a smaller shape on the ground. The smaller figure had Leon's dark curls. The shadow's "mouth" opened around the child's head like it was swallowing him whole.

Theresa's stomach lurched. Elena gasped quietly into her hands.

Alex cleared his throat. "Elena, I found something new in the probate records yesterday. Theresa, sorry I didn't think to mention it earlier."

She shook her head. "Doesn't matter. What'd you find?"

"Clara Whitaker wasn't the only heir. She had an older brother, Darryl. He was declared legally dead several years after Clara vanished. There was no body found, same as her. The estate then passed to distant cousins, finally into a trust, and that's when your parents entered the scene, Elena. But the trust documents list Darryl as 'presumed deceased due to disappearance under mysterious circumstances'—the same night as Clara."

Elena stared at him. "My mother never talked about there being two kids, only that the family had bad luck.

She called it the 'Whitaker curse.' Said that anyone who tried to leave the house or sell it paid a price. I thought it was just old-lady superstition."

Leon looked up from his drawing. "The shadow ate the man Darryl too. I saw him in the basement. In my dream. He was trying to warn me, but the dark took his mouth."

A cold draft swept through the room. Every light flickered once, hard. The portraits on the stairwell seemed to lean forward.

***

Theresa's phone buzzed in her pocket. She pulled it out, expecting Jasmine or Mia. Instead, it was an email from an unknown contact.

Subject: *Stop shading the truth.*

The body was one single line.

"Leave the manor alone, or the shadows take what's yours next."

She showed the screen to Alex. His jaw tightened. "Elena, we're going to leave. Now. Do you have Leon's bag?"

They gathered the children quickly, and Elena produced a duffel bag that looked stuffed to the gills. Emily clutched her castle drawing, and Leon refused to let go of the newest shadow picture, folding it into his pocket like a lucky token. As they hurried toward the front door, the floorboards groaned louder, almost in protest.

Outside, the sky had darkened to a bruised purple. Theresa glanced back at the manor. In the uppermost turret window, a silhouette stood motionless. It was tall, dark, and looked as if it was watching them.

Elena crouched down to Leon's level, resting her hands on his shoulders. "Remember what we talked about, Leon. You'll be as safe as safe can be with Miss T and Mr. Alex. It's only for a couple of days. Have fun with Emily, and at daycare. I'll see you real soon, buddy." She wrapped her arms around his slender shoulders, holding him tight. "I'll see you soon."

She stood and helped him into the car, fussing with the booster seat for a moment before Leon said, "I have my picture of Mom and Daddy. I'll be fine, Auntie."

"I know you will." She bent close and dropped a gentle kiss on his temple. "Love you."

"Love you too."

In the car, Emily fell asleep almost immediately, exhausted by all the excitement. Photo in hand, Leon stared out the window, silently watching something only he could see.

That night, after tucking both children into their beds, Leon on a foldout cot beside Emily, Theresa sat with Alex on their couch, laptop open. The threatening email sat in her inbox like an open wound.

Emily stirred in her sleep, whimpering. Theresa heard her and went to her side. The girl thrashed once, then sat bolt upright, eyes wide and glassy.

"Momma T," she whispered, voice small. "The shadows came in my dream. They were playing hide-and-seek, but they didn't want to be found. They took Leon behind the curtain. And then they said my name. They said, 'Emily's next.'"

Theresa pulled her close. "It was just a dream, witchling. We're safe here."

But as she rocked Emily back to sleep, Theresa looked toward the window. The streetlamp outside flickered. Beneath it, she was certain she saw a patch of darkness that stood too tall, and far too still.

She didn't blink this time.

***

The Willow Creek Public Library stood like a sentinel on Main Street, its redbrick facade adorned with whimsical gargoyles that seemed to wink in the afternoon sun. Theresa slipped through the heavy oak doors, the familiar scent of aged paper and polished wood enveloping her like an old friend. It was lunchtime, or as close to it as her daycare schedule allowed, and she'd managed to sneak away for what she and Alex had dubbed a "research lunch." Mia had promised to hold down the fort, with Jasmine and Sarah leading a sing-along to keep the chaos at bay.

Theresa's phone buzzed in her pocket, a reminder of the world she'd left behind, but for now, she pushed it aside. This was about Leon's drawings, Elena's plea, and the shadows that refused to stay buried.

Alex was waiting in the reference section, his domain of dusty tomes and humming microfiche machines. He looked up from a stack of film reels, his eyes lighting up behind his glasses. "There you are, Mrs. Daye-Reed. I was starting to think you'd been waylaid by a glitter emergency."

Theresa grinned, sliding into the chair beside him. "Close. Milo declared war on the crayon bin. But Mia's got it under control." She leaned in, her shoulder brushing his, and planted a quick kiss on his cheek. "So, research lunch? Did you pack sandwiches, or are we surviving on suspense?"

He chuckled, his ears turning that endearing shade of pink she loved. "Suspense it is, with a side of history. I pulled the old *Willow Creek Gazette* archives, microfiche from the 1950s through the 2000s, digitized after that. If Shadowbrook Manor has secrets, they'll be here in the older information." He threaded a reel into the machine, the soft whir filling the quiet alcove. The screen flickered to life, casting a pale glow on their faces.

Theresa watched as headlines scrolled by, touting town fairs, local elections, and even the occasional scandal. But Alex knew his way around these relics and followed clues like they were a map to buried treasure. "Elena's story about the estate got me thinking," he said, advancing the film. "The Whitaker family. They owned it for generations. There was the disappearance in the '70s, Clara Whitaker, Darryl's sister. She vanished during a family gathering. The papers called her a runaway, but rumors said otherwise."

The screen settled on a grainy article from 1974: "Local Heiress Vanishes from Family Estate—Foul Play Suspected?"

Theresa leaned closer, her hand finding Alex's under the table. "Look at this. 'Witnesses reported strange shadows lurking in the gardens, as if the house itself was watching.' Shadows. Just like Leon's drawings."

Alex nodded, his thumb tracing circles on her palm, the connection a small, flirty distraction amid the tension. "Creepy, right? But here's the clue." He zoomed in on a faded photo accompanying the article: Shadowbrook Manor in its heyday, turrets piercing the sky, shaped and edged hedges framing the grounds. In the foreground, a group of people posed stiffly, but in the background, blurred shapes loomed near the windows. There were indistinct figures that could be tricks of the light or something more sinister. Scrawled in the caption: "The estate's 'watching shadows' have long fueled local lore."

Theresa's skin prickled, the connection too stark to ignore. "That matches Leon's sketches, those tall, indistinct watchers. If Clara's disappearance ties into this, maybe the family's feuds go deeper than Elena knows. Inheritance, cover-ups..."

Alex advanced to another reel, but his free hand wandered to her knee, squeezing gently. "You're brilliant, you know that? Turning kid art into detective work." His voice dropped to a whisper, laced with that bookish charm. "But if we're playing Nancy Drew and the Hardy Boy, I insist on a romantic subplot."

She laughed softly, glancing around to ensure no patrons were nearby. The library was quiet, save for the distant rustle of pages. "Oh? And what's that entail?"

He feigned seriousness, pulling a slim children's book from his pocket. It was a battered copy of *The Day the Crayons Quit*. "Well, for starters, a dramatic reading." Clearing his throat, he opened to a random page, adopting exaggerated voices. "'Dear Duncan, I'm tired of being the background! Love, Black Crayon—who's great for shadows, by the way.'" His imitation of a whiny crayon had Theresa stifling giggles, but when he got to the part about the crayons rebelling, his cheeks flushed pink. "Okay, maybe not my best performance. But see? Even crayons have shadows, and they find their way back to the box."

Theresa's heart swelled, the moment a perfect balm to the mystery's chill. She cupped his face, pulling him in for a kiss that lingered just long enough to make him blush deeper. "You're adorable when you go all librarian on me. But seriously, this photo? I think it's a lead. We should show Elena."

Alex nodded, powering down the machine. "Agreed. But first, promise me there'll be no storming the manor without backup. We've got Emily to think about, and…well, us." His eyes softened, the flirtation giving way to genuine concern. "I love our adventures, but I love coming home to you more."

She squeezed his hand, the weight of the clue tempered by his warmth. "Deal. Together, always."

As they gathered their printouts, a copy of the article and the eerie photo, Theresa's phone buzzed insistently. She pulled it out, scanning the texts from Mia. *Twins are napping like angels. Milo tried to "help" with snack prep, there are apple slices everywhere. LOL. How's research? Need me to stay late?*

Theresa typed back quickly: *Research gold. Shadows confirmed creepy. Back soon. Thanks for holding the fort! Hugs to the chaos crew.* She hit Send, then pocketed the phone with a smile. The daycare was her anchor, and Mia her rock. Whatever shadows awaited at Shadowbrook, they'd face them with light. And maybe a few crayons for good measure.

Chapter Seven

The Willow Creek Police Station hadn't changed much in the months since she'd been there last. She could still smell that faint whiff of burnt coffee and hear the electric noise of the flickering fluorescents. Theresa sat across from Officer Daniels, a printout of the anonymous email sitting on the desk between them. Alex flanked her, his hand warm on her knee under the table.

"Shadows in drawings? Threatening emails?" Daniels sighed, rubbing his stubbled chin. "Kids imagine things, Mrs. Daye-Reed. And trolls love blogs. Spam isn't quite a B&E, you know. Change your passwords, enable moderation."

Theresa leaned forward, voice steady. "Already done and done. This isn't my first rodeo, Officer Daniels. This isn't just imagination. Leon's parents died suspiciously, and these shadows match the manor's history. Please, at least look into Shadowbrook."

Daniels glanced at the drawing she'd brought, a car wreathed in pursuing shadows, and shrugged. "Coincidences. But file a report if it makes you feel better."

"You know I will," she said with a smile as she pushed to her feet. Alex went with her as she made her way to the reception desk.

"Was he this way last time?" Alex asked.

"Worse, I think. Though I've got some influence with him because of the way everything turned out with Emily." She shook her head. "He should know from experience that he can't get rid of me so easily."

Theresa left the station with a thin manila folder stamped *INCIDENT REPORT* and a growing knot of frustration. Alex drove them home in silence for the first few blocks, then reached over and squeezed her hand.

"He's not wrong about trolls," he said quietly. "But he's also not looking hard enough. We'll have to do it ourselves. The duo rides again."

Theresa nodded. "Tonight. The manor's archives. Elena gave me a couple of keys for 'emergencies.' I do believe this qualifies. I'll drop her a text and let her know we're out there once we're inside."

"Smart, if paranoid. That won't give her an opportunity to give anyone a heads-up that an investigation is commencing." He squeezed her hand. "I don't think she's part of any cover-up, if that weighs in her favor."

"It does, and neither do I. Just wanting to be really careful here."

"My smart wife. Love you, T."

"Love you, my husband. And you're pretty intelligent your own self." She smiled at him. "Love you so much."

That evening, after tucking Emily and Leon into their sleeping arrangements with extra night-lights and Emily's protector-shadow drawing taped between them, Theresa and Alex slipped out, leaving the sleeping children in Mia's care. She'd agreed for her and Milo to stay over, pulling "emergency auntie duty," keeping the house bright and locked.

To Theresa, the drive on the highway leading out to where Shadowbrook sat felt like it took much longer in the dark, the headlights cutting narrow tunnels through the looming trees.

"I want to stop before we get there. If it's a person terrorizing Leon, then we need to take them by surprise."

"Agreed," Alex said, slowing the car. "And also not paranoid at all."

"Stop." She grinned, then stuck her tongue out at him. "I'm smart, remember?"

"I'll never forget."

They parked a quarter mile down the access road and walked the rest of the distance, about half a mile, under moonlight, keeping their flashlights off to avoid drawing attention. The manor loomed blacker than the night around it. One key fit the side door as promised. Inside, the house breathed differently after dark. The creaks were sharper, the stale air colder, and every shadow deeper.

Theresa pulled out her phone and sent the precomposed text to Elena. *Alex and I are going to root around in the study at Shadowbrook. We'll let you know if we find anything of note.*

She got a response almost immediately: *Be careful out there. Let me know when you're out safely.*

Will do.

Theresa lifted her head and glanced at Alex. "Done. Remind me to text her when we're back in the car."

They headed straight for the second-floor study Elena had mentioned. It was a locked room at the end of the east wing that had once been Clara Whitaker's office for her work on the estate. This key turned with a reluctant click. Inside, dust sheets draped over furniture like ghosts while shelves sagged under leather-bound ledgers and boxes of yellowed correspondence.

Alex switched on a small LED lantern they'd brought with them, keeping the beam low. They worked in silence, sorting through drawers and files. Most were mundane tax records and old deeds, but in a cedar box under the desk (the lock already pried open years ago), they found a bundle of letters tied with faded ribbon.

The top one was addressed to Clara in looping script: "My dearest sister, the shadows grow restless. Do not sign the papers. They'll take more than the house."

No signature, just initials: D.W.

Darryl Whitaker.

Theresa opened the next letter, dated two days before Clara's disappearance:

"The developers press harder. Horizon promises riches, but I've seen what waits by the well after dark. The shadows will not forgive betrayal of blood. If I vanish, know it was not by choice."

Alex's voice was low. "Darryl knew something. Warned her. Then both were gone the same night."

They photographed every page with their phones, hands steady despite the chill crawling up their spines. As they repacked the box, a floorboard groaned with a step, though their feet were motionless. They froze. Nothing moved. But the house felt like it was awake now, listening.

They left quickly, locking the study behind them, hearts hammering. Theresa glanced over her shoulder, half expecting to see the figure again, but the window was just dark with shadows.

Headed home, she sent as promised once they were back outside.

Thank you for letting me know, Elena responded.

***

The next morning at Sunnybrook, Leon was pale and quiet. During art time, he chose only black and gray crayons, drawing without pause. When Theresa knelt beside him, he pushed the paper toward her without looking up.

A winding road under a stormy sky. A small car was speeding away. Behind it, a single enormous shadow, longer than the road itself, was racing in pursuit, tendrils stretching toward the taillights like grasping hands. In the driver's seat, two stick figures: one with long hair like Leon's mother, one with a beard like his father. The shadow's "mouth" was open wide.

Theresa's breath caught. "Leon, is this the night they went away?"

He nodded once, eyes glassy. "They were arguing. About the house. The shadows followed them to the airport. Then the plane…" He trailed off, shoulders hunching. "They chased the car first. I saw it in my dream. Same as the basement."

Theresa hugged him gently. "We're going to stop them, sweetheart. I promise."

Mia found Theresa in the kitchen later, her expression filled with tension. "Javi was dropping off supplies here this morning. He says he saw a dark van idling at the curb across from the daycare. It had tinted windows, no plates visible. It was there when he brought the stuff inside and was still there twenty minutes later when he was leaving. It peeled out when he started walking toward it. Looked deliberate."

Theresa's stomach twisted. "No plates? Was it a van or an SUV?"

"Could be either. But Javi said the driver was watching the rainbow door like he was waiting for someone to come out."

That afternoon, Theresa checked *Kid Quips*. The *Friendly Shadows* post had gained even more traction, but the comments section had taken a darker turn. Amid the sweet parent stories sat new anonymous entries:

"Some shadows chase faster than cars. Ask the pilot." —*HorizonGhost*

"You found the letters. Cute. But reading them won't bring anyone back. Stop before the next crash." —*D.W.*

"Leon draws what he remembers. You should ask what *else* he saw that night." —*NoName299*

Theresa's hands shook as she screenshotted them. The initials D.W. matched the letters. Coincidence? Or someone playing a very cruel game?

She texted Alex about the latest concerns. *We have blog comments referencing the letters. And D.W. initials. They know we were there last night.*

His reply came instantly. *Coming to the cottage as soon as I can. Don't leave the building.*

As the day wound down, Theresa watched the children play, Emily trying to coax Leon into a game of shadow puppets with the overhead projector. For a moment, Leon smiled when Emily's dragon puppet "breathed" light across his dark drawing. It might have been heartbreakingly small and tentative, but it was a smile. That alone felt like a win.

But outside the wide windows, the afternoon sun stretched the trees' shadows long and thin across the lawn. One shadow, near the fence, seemed to linger longer than the rest. Taller. Watching.

Theresa turned the projector brighter.

The shadow didn't shrink.

It simply waited.

When Alex arrived, Theresa had Mia recount what Javi had told her. He pressed his lips together until they were pale, and his worried eyes gazed at Theresa while he listened. As she'd expected, he had an action plan almost immediately.

"Let's aim one of the regular security cameras so it picks up where that van was parked. That'll make me feel better. If we catch it on film, then that's something we can take to Daniels."

Then Alex put action to his words, and within twenty minutes, things were arranged the way he wanted. He found Theresa and kissed her softly, telling her, "Sorted."

That night, back at home, Emily and Leon slept curled under the same blanket, night-lights shining a constellation on the ceiling. Theresa sat at the kitchen table with Alex, prints of the photographed letters spread between them like evidence.

"We're getting closer," Alex said. "But so are they."

"We just have to get there first." Theresa shrugged like it was no big deal, pulling a grin from a very grim Alex.

***

Theresa picked up her phone, reading through the script she and Alex had quickly put together. She called Willow Development Corp, the company that Melanie had worked for, and the one that had pushed her and Elena to sell the home as-is.

"Hello?" someone—likely the receptionist—answered.

Theresa didn't know what she'd expected, but this wasn't that.

"Good morning. This is Willow Development Corp., correct? I'm Theresa Reed, and I'd like to book an appointment with someone to talk about investment opportunities."

"Hello, Ms. Reed. What type of investments are you considering? I want to ensure I place you with the right resource."

"Real estate opportunities. I've seen the signs around town, and it looks like your firm turns a fair bit of homes. I'd like to learn more about that aspect of the business." Theresa was glad they'd done a script, because with that in mind, she'd been able to answer the woman's question easily.

"I understand. I have an opening at six o'clock tomorrow, if that would suit?"

"Yes, that would be fine. Can you tell me who the appointment is with? Just so I come in knowing the right name."

"Yes, ma'am. Mr. Nielsen will be awaiting your arrival. He's our expert on real estate investment."

"Perfect. Thank you."

Theresa hung up and looked at Alex, who was beaming as if she'd done a one-woman play flawlessly. "I'm glad I was ready."

"I think you would have been fine regardless, but it is fun to know we could predict their questions so well."

She nodded. "Okay, tomorrow is the fun day at the cottage. I need to finish a few more batches of cookies. Wanna help?"

He stood and pulled her up, wrapping an arm around her shoulders. "I'd love to be your sous chef, T. Lead on, oh leader."

Chapter Eight

The garden at Sunnybrook Cottage burst with summer energy for the inaugural "Imagination Day" fair. Booths were lined up along the back fence of the playground. Each had a different fun offering—face paint, puppet shows, make your own stickers, sidewalk chalk—and there was even a gigantic bounce house groaning under kid weight.

Theresa manned the sidewalk art station, her sundress dusted with chalk, as Elena and Leon arrived, the boy holding his aunt's hand. He'd gone back to her apartment yesterday, as both women acknowledged him staying with Theresa and Alex wasn't a long-term solution.

"Welcome to the fun zone," Theresa said, handing Leon a bright yellow piece of chalk. "Draw something pretty today?"

Leon nodded hesitantly, but when Jasmine started the shadow puppet show, silhouettes dancing on a sheet, his face paled and he shouted, "No! The shadows are coming!" He bolted, running into the building and hiding behind the rainbow door, tears streaming down his little face.

Theresa dropped her chalk and hurried after him, Elena close behind. Leon pressed his back flat against the painted wood, eyes squeezed shut, hands over his ears as though he could block out the laughter and applause from the puppet stage.

"Leon, sweetheart, it's just puppets," Theresa said, kneeling to his level. "Light and hands. Nothing real."

He shook his head violently. "They're not pretend. They're watching. They saw the kids and came closer. They want to play again."

The puppet show had paused as Jasmine peeked around the sheet, concerned. Parents murmured, some smiling indulgently about imagination running wild, but Elena's face was tight with worry. She scooped Leon up, murmuring apologies, and carried him to the quiet corner near the reading nook inside the cottage.

Theresa mouthed, "It's okay," to Jasmine, then followed Elena. "He's been triggered before by shadows moving," she said softly. "The projector and the dancing puppets sounds like it's too much like the 'games' he talks about."

Elena rocked Leon gently. "I thought a community day would help. Normal kid stuff. But every time the light shifts..." She trailed off, eyes glistening. "He's getting worse, not better."

Leon lifted his head just enough to whisper, "They followed us here. From the manor. They like crowds. Easier to hide."

Theresa exchanged a concerned look with Elena. The fair continued outside, where the day was filled with music, giggles, and the bounce house creaking, but inside the cottage, the air felt thinner, the shades of gray more watchful.

***

Later that day, after the last families had trickled away and the garden had been tidied, Theresa drove to the offices of Willow Development Corp. The building sat on the newer edge of town, all glass and steel, a sharp contrast to Shadowbrook's ivy-choked stone. Alex had spent the previous night digging through public records and old business filings. They both felt that the connections were there, faint but unmistakable.

The waiting room smelled of fresh carpet and printer ink. A receptionist offered bottled water. When Mr. Nielsen appeared, Theresa stood with her hand out, and he shook it firmly. Nielsen was a fit man in his mid-forties, wearing a tailored suit and giving her a practiced smile. Gesturing to the doorway, he ushered Theresa into a corner office with floor-to-ceiling windows overlooking a manicured corporate campus.

"Ms. Reed, pleasure to meet you. Looking to invest? We have prime parcels near the old Whitaker estate—Shadowbrook Manor, they call it now. Scenic views, redevelopment potential."

Theresa kept her tone light. "Actually, I've heard rumors about Shadowbrook. Family disputes, stalled sales, that sort of thing. Is the property still on the market?"

Nielsen's smile didn't falter, but his eyes flickered, quick as a shadow crossing sunlight. "Old estates always come with stories. The current owners, I believe they're distant heirs, are motivated to sell. We've been in preliminary talks. The property has a clean title, no major liens. Just the usual small-town gossip."

Theresa leaned forward slightly. "Gossip about developers pressuring families? Or about the place being difficult to develop?"

He laughed, short and controlled. "Every historic property has a 'haunted' angle for the locals. Boosts tourism, honestly. But no, nothing unusual. Horizon Properties, our parent company, specializes in sensitive redevelopment. We respect history while moving forward."

Theresa noted the name drop. *Horizon again*. She pressed gently. "And the Whitaker heirs? Any resistance?"

Nielsen's pen tapped once against his desk in clear annoyance. "Oh, there aren't any. The property was acquired by a different family a few decades ago. As far as we know from the new owners, there's one cousin who's been vocal against the sale. Thinks the place should stay untouched. Sentimental, I suppose. But a simple majority vote wins in trust matters. Our paperwork's nearly finalized."

"That's very interesting. It's also a far cry from what local sources say. Do you have an investor packet?"

This time, Nielsen bristled at the mention of local rumors. With a wave of his hand, he dismissed her. "You can pick it up at reception. Thanks for your interest, Ms. Reed."

Theresa thanked him and left, pausing to pick up the promised packet. The whole time, her pulse was flying quickly. Outside, she texted Alex: *Horizon confirmed. One cousin *not Elena* resisting. I believe Nielsen knows more than he's saying.*

Copy. I'll let Elena know what you found out.

Love you.

My Mrs. Daye-Reed, I adore you.

Theresa smiled, then used voice-to-text to send another message. *I don't know what kindness I did that I deserved an angel like you, Alex, but I'll keep you until the world stops spinning.*

***

"Hey, T, Javi noticed the Exit Express needs tightening. We're going to stay after and work on that." Mia grinned at Theresa over the tray of gluten-free chicken nuggets they were readying for the oven. "I like putting him to good use, you know?"

"There are so many undercurrents in that statement, I don't know where to start." Theresa returned Mia's smile. "Emily is going to the library today, so I can come back and chat."

"Only if you bring the wine. You're going to blab and tell us everything. We haven't even had time to debrief after Portland. We're overdue." Mia dumped another handful of nuggets on the tray, separating the frozen-together ones and spreading them for maximum crispiness.

"Sauvignon deal." Theresa turned to make the juice punch they typically had for lunch, mixing white grape and cranberry juice together into a big jug, ready for pouring. She took off her gloves, tossing them into the trash. "I think that's everything. I'll go let Jasmine and Sarah know we're ready for food in fifteen."

"Sauvignon deal." Mia held out her pinkie, then realized she still had her food gloves on. She quickly stripped them off and held out her little finger again. "Pinkie swear with me. You can't break a pinkie swear."

"I pinkie swear," Theresa said as she shook Mia's hand. "I swear, you're the neediest child we have. Did you know that?"

"Lifetime achievement award winner, right here."

After pickup, Theresa ran Emily over to the library and went in for a quick hello with Alex, letting him know she would be at the daycare for a bit longer. He gave her a sweet kiss and a covert swat on the behind.

Back at the cottage, she went in the front door to find Milo standing guard.

"Shall not pass," he yodeled, adding multiple syllables to each word.

"Does Mom know you've watched *The Lord of the Rings*?" She laughed and gave him a high five. "Great movie."

"Cartoon," he corrected her.

"Even better," she agreed. "Mom and Unka out back already?"

"Yup." He smiled up at her. "Rawr."

"Rawr."

She dropped off the wine in the refrigerator and made her way to the back door. Outside, she found Javi fiddling with the swing with a tool in his hand and Mia spread out on the ground, eyes closed, face turned toward the sun arcing toward the horizon.

"You look like you're helping," Theresa teased.

"Supervisor. Every job needs at least one."

"Then what's your job now that I'm here?" Theresa was grinning as she eased down to sit next to Mia.

"Co-director, which does not immediately mean you get the supervisor position."

"True, and I can understand why that'd be your argument." She sighed and rolled her eyes at Javi, who chuckled. "Pretty sure owner trumps co-director."

"I knew you were going to use that reasoning. What good does the job title do me, then?"

"Means you get to hire assistants, can onboard new clients, and decline a client if they prove problematic. But you don't have to do payroll, pay taxes, or have your name on the license, which means you're safe from the cost of insurance too." Theresa angled her arms behind her, stretching out a little more in the sunshine.

"I can fire an existing client? Why didn't I know that?"

"Because she knew you'd want to fire Hargrove immediately," Javi chimed in, earning a glare from Mia.

"Ouch, why aren't you on my side?" Mia sat up to glare harder at her brother. "You're supposed to be on my side. Besides, you complain about Hargrove as much as I do."

"She's harmless, though. And Landon is a bueno boy. Those new twins are a different story." Javi waved the tool around. "Battery rabbits, always hopping around."

"Their mom is super sweet, though. She knows they're a handful. I think she was glad to go back to work." Theresa laughed softly. "That's the only way she gets a rest."

"How much longer?" Milo called from the open door.

"Until I'm done," Javi called back. "We'll get a treat after, mijo."

"Okay, Tio Javi. I wait."

"Don't you have a meeting tonight?" Mia asked the question so casually that it took a couple of seconds for Theresa to realize what she meant. Javi was a recovering addict, clean now for a long time, but he still attended meetings regularly.

"Not until eight o'clock. Plenty of time to get Milo some ice cream." He removed a screw and studied it for a moment before picking up a can of spray adhesive. As he applied it to the screw, he said, "That new boy, Leon, he's carrying some dark things, isn't he?"

"His parents were killed not long ago in a plane crash," Theresa explained. "That's heavy for anyone."

Mia nodded. "His drawings are intense, you know?"

"When I started in rehab, they had us draw our feelings," Javi shared. "It was a pretty good way to purge bad mojo without having to hurt anyone's feelings. I see that in Leon. As long as he can put the feelings out in crayon, he's not hurting anyone."

"That's a great way to look at it," Theresa mused. "That family's had enough bad mojo to last a while."

"What if we got him to put a little glitter on the drawings? We can call it 'monster repellent,'" Mia suggested.

"Could be 'shadow suppression dust' too."

Javi laughed, "Boy'd probably believe both if you guys told him. He's definitely got some hero worship going on with Miss T."

Theresa shrugged. "As long as he believes I can keep him safe, I can. It's like Santa Claus that way."

"What's like Santa Claus?" Milo asked from directly behind Theresa.

She glanced at Mia, who had her lips pressed tight together, trying not to laugh. Then she looked at Javi, who had a matching expression on his face.

"Santa Claus is magic." She turned and smiled at Milo.

"Rawr. Everyone knows that."

***

That evening, Elena stopped by the house with Leon asleep on her shoulder. She looked exhausted, dark circles under her eyes deeper than usual.

"I've been thinking," she said as they sat at the kitchen table, mugs of chamomile untouched. Leon was on the living room couch. "My cousin Marcus, on my mother's side. He's the one Nielsen mentioned. He's been emailing me for months, insisting we block the sale.

Says the manor 'belongs to the family blood,' that selling it will 'wake things.' I thought he was just eccentric. He's not owed any money, because my aunt didn't buy into the property. But after Leon's meltdown today, what if he knows something? What if he's the one leaving notes, trying to scare us off?"

Theresa hesitated. "It's possible. But the threats feel colder. More calculated. Marcus sounds passionate. This feels different."

Elena rubbed her temples. "I don't know who to trust anymore. Not even my own family."

****

The phone rang at 10:47 p.m., their landline, rarely used. Theresa answered, expecting Mia or a wrong number.

Static hissed first. Then came a low, calm voice, genderless, almost pleasant.

"Theresa Daye-Reed. You've been shining lights where they don't belong."

Her grip tightened on the receiver. "Who is this?"

A soft chuckle. "The one who watches. The one who waits. You're close now. Too close. Tell the boy to stop drawing. Tell the librarian to stop reading. Or the next shadow won't chase a car—it'll chase a child."

The line went dead.

Theresa stared at the phone, heart slamming against her ribs. Alex appeared in the doorway, Emily's storybook still in his hand from bedtime.

"Who was it?"

"The watcher," she whispered. "They know who we are. They know everything."

Chapter Nine

Dinner at the Daye-Reed home was a cozy affair, spaghetti twirled on forks, Emily's latest rainbow drawing taped to the fridge. Alex passed the garlic bread, eyes on Theresa. "Tough day at the daycare?"

She shook her head, twirling her wedding ring. "No, everything's good there. I just can't stop thinking that Nielsen's hiding something about the manor. And then there's Leon's drawing of the basement, with the shadow 'swallowing' a figure. Like the missing heir."

Emily looked up from her plate, sauce on her chin. "The eating shadow? Leon told me about it. He says it only eats people who try to leave the house forever."

Alex and Theresa exchanged a glance. Their home felt a little smaller tonight, the windows darker despite the warm lamp glow.

After the dishes were done, Emily settled with a bedtime story from Alex, because he did the best voices. Then Theresa showed Alex the latest sketch Elena had texted. The basement stairs descended into black, a tall stick figure at the bottom reaching up with impossibly long arms. The shape being swallowed had Clara Whitaker's hairstyle from the portrait, hair fanning out like it was being pulled downward.

"Reenactment," Alex murmured. "Leon's never seen photos of Clara's disappearance, but he's drawing it beat for beat. Either he's channeling trauma he overheard from his parents, or something else is feeding him the images."

Theresa rubbed her arms. "Elena's convinced it's her cousin Marcus. The resistant one. She's meeting him tomorrow to confront him about the threats."

Alex frowned. "I cross-checked. Marcus was out of state the night of the plane crash. He was at a conference in Chicago, with a bunch of time-stamped photos online. And the blog comments referencing the letters? The IP trace bounced through proxies, but one pinged near the manor grounds, not Marcus's address."

"So he's not as likely," Theresa said slowly. "But then who?"

***

The next morning at Sunnybrook, Elena arrived pale but determined. "I talked to Marcus last night. He cried, Theresa. Said he's been trying to think of a way to protect the family from selling because he believes the curse is real. He swears he never sent notes, never threatened anyone. He's terrified for Leon, but I don't think he's behind anything." She handed over a printed email chain, with time stamps and locations. The same alibi evidence Alex had found.

Theresa exhaled. "Then we're looking in the wrong direction."

"Uh, Theresa, I wanted to let you know that I'm still committed to finding you and Alex the perfect location."

She reached out and pulled Elena into a hug that lasted a long time.

"That's the last thing on my mind. We've plenty of time to work on that."

Nodding, Elena kissed Leon on the temple and then headed out.

During naptime, Mia pulled Theresa aside. "Javi was here earlier working on the fence. He mentioned an old groundskeeper who still lives in the caretaker's cottage on the Shadowbrook property. Name's Raymond Hale, goes by Ray. Been there forever, even after the family left. Javi said that the locals all say the man is 'touched,' that he talks to himself like he'll answer. Javi was delivering out that way yesterday and swears he saw him near the front of the property, just standing there, watching the road."

Theresa's skin prickled. "Ray. Do you think he might be the figure in Leon's drawings? Is he tall, quiet, sticking to the background?"

Mia nodded. "Sounds right. Javi said the man's eyes followed him the whole time he was driving past. Creepy as hell."

That afternoon, Leon sat at the art table, drawing without prompting. When Theresa approached, he slid the paper over silently.

The scene was of the manor's front drive. There was a young woman, probably Clara—the hair looked right—who was running toward a waiting car. Behind her was a tall figure in a winter coat, arms outstretched. Shadows poured from the house like smoke, flowing around the tall figure and wrapping around Clara's ankles, appearing to pull her back. The car door stood open, but Clara never reached it. Leon had drawn what looked like cartoon panels. In the final one, the shadow swallowed the woman whole.

Theresa stared. "Leon, is this what happened to the lady in the pictures?"

He nodded. "A man was there. He said he tried to help, but the shadows listened to someone else. Someone who wanted her gone."

Theresa's heart thudded. "Ray Hale?"

Leon's eyes widened. "You know him?"

"We're going to find out who's really listening to the shadows, sweetheart."

***

That evening, Theresa had forgotten a folder she needed for end-of-month invoices, and with Alex already picking up Emily from a playdate, she drove back to the cottage alone. When she came back outside with the folder in hand, she realized the driver's side tire was flat. It had been slashed clean through the sidewall.

This is not a simple flat tire. There was no note, no sign of a struggle, just the single deliberate cut.

She called Alex first, then Officer Daniels. They arrived within almost simultaneously, Alex and Emily's fast footsteps beating the sweep of Daniels's flashlight across the gravel by a heartbeat.

"Could be random vandalism," Daniels said, but his tone lacked conviction this time. "Or someone sending a message. We'll dust the car, check for prints." He studied her for a long minute. "I know I don't have to tell you to stay vigilant."

Theresa nodded, but her eyes kept drifting to the darkening street. A tall figure stood under the far lamp. It looked like Ray Hale's build, coat collar up, motionless. She didn't say anything, just watched, and when Daniels turned his flashlight that way, the figure had already melted into the trees.

***

They rode home together in Alex's truck. Once back at the house, family dinner was quieter than usual. Emily twirled her favorite spaghetti slowly, sensing the mood. Alex had lit every lamp, banishing all dark corners.

After Emily was tucked in with extra night-lights and her protector drawing, the adults sat at the kitchen table, voices low.

"We need firm boundaries," Alex said. "No solo trips to the manor. No more late-night research alone. Those are absolutes. We tell Elena everything tomorrow. All that we know about Ray, the slashed tire, and Leon's reenactment drawing. And we go to Daniels with it all. This isn't coincidence anymore."

Theresa leaned into him. "I know. But Leon's drawing the truth. Someone made sure Clara never left. Someone made sure Leon's parents' plane went down. And now they're circling us."

Alex pulled her closer. "Then we circle back. Together. You and me, honey. No one goes near Shadowbrook without backup. And we keep the lights on, literal and otherwise."

Chapter Ten

Moonlight filtered through the manor's overgrown hedges as Theresa and Alex crouched in the bushes, his "just happened to have them in the truck" night vision binoculars trained on the darkened windows. "This is boundary-pushing," Alex whispered, but his grin betrayed excitement.

A figure emerged from the manor's side door, their brilliant flashlight beam cutting through the night. It looked like Ray Hale had full run of the main house. He handed a folder over to the driver of a waiting van marked with Willow Development's logo.

Theresa's breath caught. This was collusion happening right in front of them.

The van's engine idled low, lights off. Ray—tall, stooped, coat collar turned up—spoke briefly to the driver through the open window, voices too soft to carry. Then he retreated into the manor, the door clicking shut behind him. The van pulled away slowly, gravel crunching under its tires, disappearing down the access road toward town.

She asked, "I thought Hale lived in the caretaker's cottage. Why is he inside the manor?"

Alex lowered the binoculars. "That's our watcher, T. Hale's been feeding documents, or worse, to Nielsen's people. Not by light of day, but still pretty blatantly."

Theresa nodded, pulse racing. "Elena said the family trusted Ray. He's been the groundskeeper since before Clara vanished. If he's spying…"

"If he's spying, then all bets are off given who he appears to be working with."

They waited another twenty minutes, ensuring no one else emerged, then slipped back to their truck hidden down the road. On the drive home, Alex kept glancing in the rearview. "No tail. But they know we're digging. That slashed tire on your car wasn't random. They've attacked us once; there's nothing to stop them doing it a second time."

***

The next morning at Sunnybrook, Elena arrived with Leon in tow. The boy looked somehow smaller today, dark circles under his eyes, clutching the strap of his backpack like a lifeline. Theresa waited until the other children settled in circle time with Jasmine and Mia before leading Elena and Leon to the quiet reading nook.

She pulled out her phone and opened the blurry photo Alex had snapped during the stakeout, Ray's profile unmistakable even in grainy moonlight.

Elena stared, color draining from her face. "That's him. Ray Hale. Seems like a nice guy. He used to give Leon candy when he was out there with his parents. Always quiet, always watching."

Theresa knelt in front of Leon, keeping her voice gentle. "Sweetheart, can you look at this picture? Is this the man who was there the night the lady disappeared? The one the shadows listened to?"

Leon studied the image for a long, silent moment. His small finger traced a scar on Ray's cheek in the photo. "Yes. That's Ray. He stood by the well. He told the shadows to take her. I saw it in my dream again last night. He said, 'The house stays ours.'"

Elena's hand flew to her mouth. "He's been working for them. For Horizon. All this time."

Theresa felt the pieces lock into place with a cold click. She immediately texted Officer Daniels the photo, along with the blog comment screenshots and Leon's most recent reenactment drawings.

His reply came within minutes: *On my way to the station. Bring the originals. We move fast. We got a positive ID from the prints on your car.*

***

By late afternoon, Willow Creek Police, joined by state investigators, had raided the caretaker's cottage on Shadowbrook grounds. Ray Hale was taken into custody without resistance, hands cuffed behind him as he was led to a waiting cruiser. Inside the small house, officers found a locked metal box hidden beneath the floorboards.

It contained a variety of items. There were copies of old Whitaker family letters that appeared to match the ones Theresa and Alex had photographed. Also recent emails between Ray and Nielsen at Willow Development, discussing "securing the property" and "removing obstacles." There was a thumb drive with flight logs, maintenance records from the small airport Leon's parents used, and annotated notes highlighting "weak points" in the plane's preflight checks. And finally a single photo of the crashed aircraft, time-stamped hours after the incident, with a handwritten note on the back: "Problem solved. Sale can proceed."

Officer Daniels called Theresa that evening from the station. "Sabotage confirmed. Preliminary forensics show tampering with the plane's hydraulics. The damage was subtle, professional. Ray's cooperating now, claims he was 'only following orders' from Horizon. Says they promised him lifetime employment and a cut if the manor sold. He's implicating Nielsen directly. We're going to be questioning the executive tomorrow. Want in?"

"Of course we do." Theresa exhaled, relief warring with dread. "And the shadows? The threats?"

Daniels paused. "Ray swears he never sent emails or made calls. Says he 'just watched.' But someone else was involved. We're tracing the burner phone used to make that call to your landline."

"Thank you, sir. It matters a lot that you're keeping me—us—in the loop."

"Just keeping you safe, Mrs. Daye-Reed. You're a staple in the community. Gotta keep you around."

***

That night, *Kid Quips* lit up with backlash. The latest post—a gentle update about "helping children feel safe in dark corners"—drew hundreds of comments. Most were supportive, but a vicious thread emerged that made her glad she still had the blog on lockdown.

"Snitches get stitches. You ruined a good man's life." —*HorizonTruth*

"Ray was protecting the house. Now the shadows have nowhere to hide. Guess who they'll come for next?" —*ShadowKeeper*

"Keep shining your little flashlight, daycare lady. See how far the light reaches when the power goes out." —*NoName000*

Theresa moderated deliberately, deleting and blocking as they met the criteria, but the comments kept appearing—new accounts spawning like shadows at dusk. She screenshotted everything and forwarded the batch to Daniels with a text: *They're escalating.*

At home, Emily sat on her bed, night-lights plugged into each electrical outlet glowing like stars. She had drawn a new protector shadow, this one wearing a police badge. She stared at it solemnly.

"They caught Ray," Theresa told her gently. "The man who was helping the bad shadows. He won't hurt anyone anymore."

Emily squeezed her hand. "I think I still need to make more protectors. Lots of them."

Alex pulled Theresa aside in the kitchen. "It's not over. Horizon's scrambling, but someone higher up is still pulling strings. And the blog threats…they're personal. Someone's watching us watch them."

Theresa glanced toward the window. The streetlamp outside burned steady tonight, no flickering, no tall silhouette beneath it.

But the darkness beyond the circle of light felt thicker than before.

She turned back to Alex, forcing a smile. "We keep the lights on. All of them."

He nodded slowly. "And we help the kids continue to draw the truth. Until the shadows can't hide anymore."

Outside, the night deepened.

Somewhere, a new watcher waited patiently, silent, ready to step into Ray's place.

Chapter Eleven

The confrontation in Nielsen's office crackled with tension. Theresa was flanked by Officer Daniels and Alex. "Your groundskeeper's been watching us," she accused, slamming photos onto the desk.

Nielsen paled. "He went rogue. He was hired to scout, not stalk. The manor's disputed, but I swear, no foul play on my end."

Daniels crossed his arms. "We have emails, flight sabotage notes, your name on the chain. Ray Hale says you green-lit 'removing obstacles.' Did that possibly include a plane crash?"

Nielsen's polished facade cracked. He sank into his chair, hands trembling. "I never ordered murder. I needed the property cleared for redevelopment. But it needed to be done quietly. Ray was supposed to persuade. Try and light a fire under old family grudges and put gentle pressure on the heirs. Not this." He looked up, eyes desperate. "But there's someone else pulling the strings. Someone inside the family who wanted the sale forced through faster than anyone."

Theresa leaned forward. "Who?"

Nielsen hesitated, then slid a thin file across the desk. "Marcus Singleton, Ms. Vargas's cousin. He came to me months ago, begging us to wait. Said the curse was real, that selling would unleash something. He's been fighting the sale publicly. But the other heir…his half sister, Sofia Clavis. Different fathers, raised in different households, and they both kept quiet about the blood tie until the trust documents surfaced last year. She claims their branch of the family has a claim on the property. Completely false, but she kept sniffing around for any money. If the sale went through, according to her, Sofia stood to inherit a larger share if the estate sold high. She's been pushing Marcus to sign, saying it's 'for everyone's future.' But privately? She hired a consultant to dig up dirt on Elena and Marcus—any old debts, possibility of custody concerns. From the questions she's asked around, I'd say she's intending to pressure them."

Alex scanned the file. "Sofia's name isn't on any Horizon paperwork."

Nielsen gave a bitter laugh. "She's smart. She always used intermediaries. Ray was one. She apparently told him that the family curse stories would keep people scared off the property until the sale closed. That he should make it look like supernatural nonsense instead of corporate greed."

Daniels took the file. "We'll bring her in for questioning. If she orchestrated the sabotage…"

Nielsen shook his head. "She didn't cut the hydraulic lines. But she knew. And she wanted it done."

***

Back at Sunnybrook that afternoon, Elena sat in the quiet office, face ashen as Theresa relayed Nielsen's revelations.

"Marcus's half sister?" Elena whispered. "I know of her, but Sofia and I have barely spoken. Ever. She lives in Chicago and always sent birthday cards for Leon, but that's it. I thought she was just...distant. She didn't factor into anything with the property. That's why I didn't mention her. You must think I'm a fool."

"No, not a fool. Someone under unbelievable stress." Theresa placed a hand on Elena's arm. "She wanted the money. And she used the old family stories of Clara, Darryl, and the supposed curse to keep everyone afraid while Horizon moved in. Ray was her go-between."

Elena's eyes filled. "All this time, I thought the shadows were real, protecting the house. But they were just her, using fear."

Leon appeared in the doorway, holding a fresh drawing. He hesitated, then walked straight to Elena and placed it on her lap without a word.

The page showed two stick figures arguing in the manor's drawing room, one with long hair labeled Miss Sofia, the other labeled Mr. Marcus. Between them, shadows swirled like smoke, but they weren't attacking.

They were listening. One shadow had a tiny ear pressed to the wall, and the other held a phone. In the background, the well gaped open, and a faint figure that looked a lot like Ray stood beside it, watching.

Elena stared. "Leon. Did you see this?"

He nodded. "In my dream last night. They were yelling about the house. Miss Sofia said, 'Sell it or lose everything.' Mr. Marcus said, 'The shadows won't let us.' Then the shadows started whispering back. They said her name. Sofia's name. Like they were choosing sides."

Theresa knelt beside him. "The shadows were arguing too?"

Leon shook his head. "No. They were waiting for someone to tell them what to do. Like Ray did."

***

Theresa stood at the daycare's back window, gazing out over the fenced playground where the Exit Express tire swing creaked gently in the breeze. It was midafternoon, with the kids scattered during free-play time. A few were digging in the sensory garden's mint and rosemary, others chasing bubbles from Javi's latest repair job on the bubble machine. The sun cast long shadows across the grass, turning the slide into a playful giant, but after the eerie discoveries at Shadowbrook Manor, every dark patch felt like a potential threat.

She rubbed her arms, a chill prickling her skin despite the warmth. Elena's warnings about "watchers" echoed in her mind, and Leon's latest drawings of lurking figures had her on edge. Was someone really out there, spying on the cottage? One anonymous note had started it all, and now, with the inheritance disputes unraveling, paranoia crept in like fog off the river.

Movement caught her eye near the fence. There was a tall, indistinct shape shifting behind the hedges, just beyond the playground's edge. Her heart skipped. It was humanoid, cloaked in shadow, unmoving as if observing.

"Mia!" she hissed, waving her co-director over without taking her eyes off it. "Look over there, by the oak tree. Is that...someone watching?"

Mia squinted, her sarcastic edge sharp as ever. "Where? Oh, wait, yeah, I see it. Definitely a Creepy McCreeperson alert. Want me to grab the broom? Or call Daniels?"

Theresa's pulse raced. "No, let's not scare the kids. But stay here and watch me. I'll check it out." She grabbed a flashlight from the emergency kit (overkill for daylight, but it felt reassuring) and slipped out the back rainbow door, her steps quiet on the grass. The figure didn't move as she approached, its outline blurring in the dappled light. "Hello? This is private property. If you're looking for someone..."

Up close, the "watcher" resolved into...a coatrack? No, it was Javi. He straightened up from where he'd been pruning overgrown branches that spilled over the shared fence line. He was tall and lanky, his work hat casting a long shadow, tools slung over his shoulder like a makeshift cloak. He turned, startled, his face breaking into a sheepish grin.

"Miss Theresa? Didn't mean to spook ya. Just trimmin' these vines. They were pokin' into your yard. Mia asked me to tidy up the edges when I was between jobs." He held up his shears as evidence, a stray leaf tumbling to the ground.

Theresa exhaled, laughter bubbling up in relief. "Javi! I thought you were…never mind. A ghost from the past, maybe." She pocketed the flashlight, feeling foolish but glad it was benign. Javi had been a rock for Mia and Milo, his gruff demeanor hiding a soft spot for all the kids. He'd even donated a birdhouse to the playground last week.

He chuckled, wiping sweat from his brow. "Ghosts? Plenty in the cemetery, probably, but they don't cross fences. I noticed that slide looks wobbly. I'll get that on my list o' things to fix."

"Thanks, Javi. Actually, that would be great. Gotta keep the kiddos safe."

As they chatted briefly about the cottage's playground and sensory maze, Theresa's tension eased. No real watcher. Just her imagination, fueled by the mystery. But it was a reminder that shadows weren't always sinister. Sometimes they were just overgrown branches.

Back inside, Mia arched an eyebrow. "Well? Do I need to sharpen the crayons for defense?"

Theresa shook her head, smiling. "False alarm. Just Javi playing gardener. But let's keep an eye out. Better safe than shadowed."

The kids' laughter from the playground pulled her back to the present, a chorus of light chasing away the doubt. For now, the only watchers were the friendly ones in their drawings.

***

That evening at the house, Emily spread Leon's latest drawings across the living room floor like puzzle pieces. Night-lights glowed brightly, and the room felt safe despite the weight of the day.

"Look," Emily said, pointing to recurring shapes. "The eating shadow always has the same mouth—big oval, no teeth. And the chasing shadow has long fingers, like this." She traced one tendril. "But in the new one— the argument one—the shadows have ears. And phones. They're not monsters. They're spies."

Theresa blinked. "Spies?"

Emily nodded solemnly. "Like in the stories. They listen and tell secrets. But they only do what the boss says. Miss Sofia was the boss. Ray was her helper. The shadows just obeyed."

Theresa watched Emily, heart aching and swelling at once. "You're figuring this out better than any of us."

Alex joined them on the floor. "Emily's right. The 'curse' was never supernatural. It was people using old fear to cover new greed. The shadows in the drawings? I think they're memories of arguments Leon overheard or dreamed, amplified by trauma. But the real darkness was human."

Emily looked up. "So, if we tell the truth...the shadows stop?"

Alex grinned. "We draw bigger protectors. Ones with flashlights and police badges and truth spells."

Theresa pulled the two people she loved more than anything close. "We're already doing that. Every time we talk about it. Every time we shine the light."

Outside, rain began to tap the windows, soft at first, then steady. The streetlamp glowed through the drops, no tall silhouette beneath it tonight.

But Theresa knew better than to trust the quiet.

***

Later, after Emily was asleep, Theresa checked her phone. A new email from an anonymous account, but Theresa knew it came from Sofia's IP, traced by Daniels's team earlier that day:

"You think you've won.

The house still stands.

The shadows remember blood.

Tell Elena her share just got smaller."

Theresa forwarded it to Daniels without replying.

She turned off the kitchen light as Alex led her to their room, leaving only the night-lights burning in Emily's room.

The rain drummed harder.

Somewhere in the dark, the last watcher waited. Not for orders this time, but for judgment.

Chapter Twelve

Elena paced the cottage kitchenette, coffee forgotten as tears fell. "My sister didn't give a flip, but Leon's dad was obsessed with the inheritance. He argued with Melanie every chance he got. Leon must have seen it all."

Theresa set the kettle down gently, giving Elena space but staying close. The daycare was closed. Of the outside kids, only Leon remained, coloring quietly in the reading nook with Emily and Milo under Mia's watchful eye. Outside, rain streaked the rainbow door's windows, blurring the world beyond.

Elena wiped her cheeks with the back of her hand. "I don't know what to believe anymore. How can the same kind old man who gave Leon sweets also be the one who took his mother and father away from him forever?"

Theresa's voice was soft. "And Leon?"

Elena's shoulders shook. "He was barely four when his parents started refurbishing Shadowbrook. After the first few months, they fought constantly about selling. My brother-in-law, he wasn't always kind when he was angry. He yelled. Threw things. Leon hid in corners, under tables. I thought it was just marital stress. But the drawings Leon did of the shadows crowding rooms, chasing, swallowing, I think they're memories. The 'shadow people' are what he saw when his father lost control. The arguments. The fear. And then when the plane crashed…it sealed it. Every shadow became the thing that took his parents away."

Theresa reached across the counter, touching Elena's wrist. "He's been carrying that alone. The manor didn't curse anyone. It just echoed what he already knew."

Elena nodded, tears coursing down her cheeks. "I should have seen it sooner. I thought the drawings were grief, not trauma reenacted."

"I told you about Dr. Macy. She's truly gifted when it comes to helping our little loves. I would recommend you call her and put a date on the calendar, and with something like that, sooner is better. You only want the best for Leon."

"I do." She turned and looked to where he sat with the two other kids, a smile on his face and a crayon a shade brighter than black in his hands. "I truly do."

***

Daniels arrived at dusk with a search warrant and a small team. The manor stood silent under heavy clouds, windows dark as empty eyes. Ray Hale, who was still in custody, had given a partial statement, probably trying to barter down the time his infractions would garner, but he dug his heels in against the accusation that he'd killed Leon's parents. He claimed Sofia had paid him to stage "hauntings," to plant fear so the family would sell quickly. But he'd also mentioned a hidden room in the basement, boarded up since the '70s, where Darryl had kept records of the family's financial ruin.

The officers pried open a false panel behind the old coal chute. Inside was a narrow chamber lit by only a single bare bulb when they found the switch. Dust coated everything, from the ledgers, to photographs, and a locked diary with Clara's name embossed on the cover.

Alex, allowed on scene as a historical consultant, opened the diary first, reading entries from 1974:

"Darryl wants the money now. Says the house is bleeding us dry. I told him no. The shadows here aren't ghosts. They're secrets. If we sell, they'll come out."

The final entry was dated the night she had vanished: "He's coming down the stairs. Lights flickering. I hear my brother shouting. If I don't make it out, tell them the well hides more than water."

Beside the diary sat a metal box. Inside: bank statements showing Darryl siphoning funds, forged signatures, and a single Polaroid of Clara at the well's edge, Darryl behind her, hand raised. It had a date stamp from the night of her disappearance. No body had ever been found, but the photo placed them both there.

Daniels sealed the evidence. "Everything looks as Hale said, including the picture he took that night. This ties Darryl to Clara's fate. And Sofia knew. It appears her consultant dug up similar records years ago. She used them to try and push your brother-in-law into selling, because if everything was made public, there are Whitaker relatives who may have argued they had a claim on the property. When he resisted...we think she had the plane disabled."

Theresa, standing in the doorway with Elena, felt the house exhale—as though a long-held breath had finally released.

***

That night, Sunnybrook Cottage became a temporary safe house. Mia had set up cots in the reading nook; night-lights formed a glowing perimeter around the children's sleeping area. Leon had refused to go back to Elena's apartment. "There are too many corners," he said. So Elena stayed, too, curled on a beanbag nearby.

Emily sat cross-legged beside Leon's cot, both children in pajamas, flashlights in hand.

"Tell me again about the shadows," she whispered.

Leon traced patterns on his blanket. "They weren't real monsters. They were Daddy when he yelled. And the dark when I hid. And Mom when she talked about money on the phone. They just...somehow they got bigger in my head."

Emily nodded wisely. "Then we make them smaller. Like this." She clicked her flashlight on, shining it across the wall. Their shadows danced, tall at first, then shrinking as she moved the beam closer. "See? Light wins. Always."

Leon watched, then reached for his sketchpad. For only the second time in weeks, he chose yellow and blue crayons instead of black.

Theresa watched from the doorway, Alex beside her.

"She's helping him," Theresa murmured. "One drawing at a time."

Alex slipped an arm around her waist. "And we're interpreting the rest. Sofia will be in custody tomorrow. Horizon's pulling out of the deal—there's just too much heat. The manor will go into protected trust status until the investigations close. No sale. No development."

Theresa leaned into him. "Leon can visit without fear. Maybe even play in the garden someday."

Outside, the rain had stopped. Moonlight slipped through the clouds, touching the rainbow door in soft silver. No tall silhouette waited under the streetlamp tonight.

Only ordinary shadows, small and harmless, stretching across the lawn.

Inside, two children whispered secrets to their flashlights.

A protector shadow, drawn in bright gold, hung above Leon's cot, smiling down.

***

"Hello," Theresa answered her cell phone without looking to see the caller.

"Mrs. Daye-Reed, it's Detective Kowalski. There has been additional information that's come to light in the Shadowbrook investigations. I think you're going to want to be out there on-site first thing in the morning."

"What? Can you tell me?"

"Not until it's been confirmed. But you seem to have a head for mysteries. I'd love to pick your brain after...well, after. Will you come?"

"Try and keep me away."

He laughed and she grinned, shaking her head at Alex's puzzled expression.

"See you tomorrow, then."

She disconnected the call and looked at Alex, a thousand ideas buzzing around in her head.

"What was that?" he asked.

"That was Detective Kowalski, inviting us to go to Shadowbrook in the morning to watch them find something."

"Find something? Like what?"

Theresa shrugged. "We'll know more tomorrow. I need to get Mia to open the cottage. I'm not going to miss this for the world."

Chapter Thirteen

Even in the daylight, the alternating lights painted the wall of trees lining the back edge of the garden red and blue. It was quiet as investigators entered Shadowbrook's basement, Theresa once again watching from afar, this time with Alex's arm around her. Forensic researchers had been poring over Clara's diary, and they'd found a vital note glued into the back cover of the book. It spoke of the existence of a second hidden room. That's why they were all here now.

Theresa tightened her grip on Alex's sleeve as officers emerged carrying sealed evidence bags. Kowalski approached them across the wet gravel, expression grim but steady.

"Darryl Whitaker didn't vanish in '74," he said without preamble. "He was killed—looks like blunt force to the skull—and his body concealed in the basement. We'll wait for the official word from the science guys, of course. Clara's diary ended the night of her last day here, but there were so many things not solved when we found her remains at the bottom of the well. The family covered up her murder in an attempt to protect the inheritance. Later, after Darryl was declared missing, both cases went cold." He looked down for a moment, then up and into Theresa's eyes. "And I've got more news about Leon's parents' accident."

"Is it good news?"

He shook his head. "I wouldn't call it that."

Theresa's stomach dropped. "What happened to his parents? They're dead, right?"

Kowalski nodded. "Melanie is dead. Ronald isn't. When Horizon started aggressively contacting them with intent, he saw a chance to cash out. Get enough money to set him up for life. But then Sofia popped up, and she pushed too hard. She threatened to expose the old crime scene if he didn't cooperate, promised to bring Whitaker relatives out of the woodwork. So he faked his death in the plane crash. Sabotaged it himself, then deliberately missed the flight and left his wife to die. The state boys finally told us they found only two victims in the wreckage, along with a melted burner phone and a single piece of paper with a surname on it. That gave us a start on finding him. He's been living off-grid in Montana. State police are en route out there to apprehend him now. It'll be interesting to see what he gained in all the madness he caused. I surely can't put a reason to any of it."

Alex exhaled slowly. "The shadows Leon drew...they were memories of his father's rage. The chasing shadow on the road, the plane crash. Even the eating shadow and the well. All of it was real, just...human."

Kowalski glanced toward the manor. "Ray Hale's already in custody for property damage, stalking, and conspiracy to defraud. We know he fed Nielson and Sofia intel and staged hauntings to try and scare the family into selling. Nielsen's facing fraud and accessory charges for the corporate side of things. Sofia's cooperating fully. She claims she only wanted the money, never murder. But Leon's father? He's the architect. The real killer."

***

The next morning, Sunnybrook Cottage felt different, sunnier, as though the rainbow door itself had brightened. Elena sat at the low art table with Leon, both of them coloring side by side. No black crayons today. Leon chose green for the lawn, blue for the sky, yellow for the sun.

Theresa knelt beside them. "Detective Kowalski needs to speak with you soon, Leon. Not in person if you don't want, though. Dr. Macy says you can always talk just through drawings. Anything you remember about your dad, the arguments, the night the plane went away. It'll help make sure no one else gets hurt."

Leon nodded without looking up. "I can draw it. The truth. Like Emily said."

He worked steadily for nearly an hour. When he finished, he slid three sheets across the table.

The first was of a tall man, his father, arguing with another man in the basement. Ray Hale.

The second was the same tall man hovering behind a woman, shadows pooling at his feet. They might not be monsters, but grief and fear were made visible.

The third was the car on a dark road, the man alone in the driver's seat, looking back as a plane exploded in the sky behind him. No chasing shadow this time, just the man's own face, twisted with something like regret.

Elena covered her mouth, tears silent. "He saw everything. And he carried it."

Theresa hugged Leon gently. "You're so brave, kiddo. This helps. A lot."

***

That night, Elena and Leon were at the Maple Street house for a low-key evening of games. The kids were the directors, picking games in turn. They were four or five selections into the night when Leon decided on shadow puppets. Theresa turned to Elena in surprise, only to see a matching expression on shock on Elena's face.

"Sure, buddy," said Alex. "Em, run get the big flashlight. The one we use for sleepouts in the backyard."

Emily was on her feet in a flash, racing to the hallway closet where all the camping gear was kept.

"Here," she said brightly, handing the flashlight to Leon. "You can be the sun." She twisted her fingers together. "I'll be the bird flying in the sunshine." Leon aimed the flashlight at her hands and the shadow

126

appeared on the wall opposite, wings flapping slowly as Emily moved her fingers. "That's so cool."

"It is," he agreed, a tiny smile on his face.

Alex said, "I can do a bunny." He fit his hands together, holding two crooked fingers up for ears, and hopped along the beam of light.

"We had a bunny in the backyard that Mommy would let me feed. Sometimes. He was cute." Leon smiled wider. "I liked that. I saw a bunny at the shadow place. Maybe if we go back, I can feed him, Auntie?"

Elena nodded. "Leon, I'd buy two bags of feed if that's what you want to do."

"I like bunnies too," Emily said. "I could come feed them with you. That way if there are two bunnies, we can feed both without playing favorites."

"That'd be good." Leon leaned against Emily's side. "You're a good friend."

"So are you." She leaned into him as well.

"There's a book at the library about bunnies that I could bring and read." Alex kept his bunny hopping around the beam of light. "It's about a baby bunny who wants a sweater and his search for someone to make him one. I won't spoil it for you, but he gets what he wants, a little closer to home."

"Home," Emily echoed, looking around the living room happily.

"Home is good," Leon said, moving to sit on Elena's lap.

"Home," Alex agreed. "Next pick for a game?"

"Go Fish," Emily shouted, vaulting up from the floor and dashing to the game caddy in the corner of the room. "Gooooo fishies."

***

Two weeks later, the arrests were complete. Ronald Latham, Leon's father, was taken into custody from inside a remote cabin outside Bozeman. He confessed within hours, claiming the crash was meant to look like an accident so he could disappear with enough money to start over. He'd cashed out their entire savings and stocks over the few weeks prior to the crash. His wife had refused to leave, so he'd made the choice for both of them.

Shadowbrook Manor was sealed pending probate reform. The trust would be restructured under court supervision, with proceeds earmarked for Leon's future and a small historical preservation fund. Elena had surrendered her rights to the property so they would pass to Leon. There would be no development, and until Leon reached adulthood, there would be no sale. The house and property would stand quiet, and probably empty, but was no longer a weapon.

At home that evening, dinner was simple. Theresa had made pancakes for dinner, because Emily declared it "victory food." Leon sat between Emily and Elena, fork sticky with syrup.

Kowalski had stopped by earlier with a small badge-shaped sticker for each child that labeled them as a "Junior Truth-Teller." Leon wore his proudly on his shirt.

Alex raised his orange juice in a mock toast. "To the light winning. And to no more shadows chasing anyone."

Emily clinked her glass against his. "And to protector shadows! They helped too."

Leon smiled. It might have been small, but it was real, the first unguarded one Theresa had seen from him. "They're not chasing anymore. They're just resting."

***

Later, after Elena and Leon had gone back to their temporary residence in a hotel suite until they could find a different apartment, Emily was tucked in, and Theresa and Alex stood at the window. The streetlamp glowed steady. No dark figure beneath it, only ordinary night, soft and unthreatening.

Theresa leaned against Alex. "Think the manor will ever feel safe again?"

He kissed the top of her head. "For Leon? Someday. Elena will take him back out there when he's ready. Show him the garden, the turret, the well, boarded and sealed. They'll turn the shadows back into ordinary shapes."

She nodded. "And we'll keep drawing the truth. Until every corner is bright."

In their living room, two night-lights burned.

Above Emily's bed hung her latest drawing, a golden protector shadow standing guard, flashlight in one hand, crayon in the other.

It smiled out at them all.

Outside, Willow Creek slept under a clear sky.

The manor waited on the edge of town, silent, but no longer hungry.

And at Sunnybrook Cottage, the rainbow door gleamed, promising tomorrow would be full of light.

Chapter Fourteen

The courthouse buzzed as new faces filled the defendant seats. Theresa sat with Elena, studying the differences from the last time she was here. The DA was still the scrappy Alma Ramirez who she'd worked with on the Pike murder case. When Ramirez caught sight of Theresa, she got a tiny smile and an up nod of acknowledgment. Theresa dipped her chin in response.

The courtroom smelled of polished wood and old paper, sunlight slanting through tall windows in dusty beams. Ronald Latham sat at the defense table in an ill-fitting suit, eyes downcast. Beside him, Sofia Clavis stared straight ahead, expression blank. Ray Hale and Mr. Nielsen were in chairs behind the table, handcuffs glinting under fluorescent lights.

The judge read the charges for each defendant in measured tones, beginning with first-degree murder, conspiracy to commit murder, fraud, stalking, and evidence tampering. Pleas followed one by one.

Ronald entered guilty to all counts, voice flat.

Sofia pleaded no contest, face wet with silent tears. Ray Hale took a plea deal for testimony against the others in exchange for reduced time. Nielsen followed suit, claiming he'd been "misled by aggressive family dynamics."

Theresa squeezed Elena's hand as the judge set sentencing dates. Leon's three drawings, carefully mounted and labeled, were entered as People's Exhibits A, B, and C. The courtroom fell quiet when the prosecutor displayed them on the screen: the basement argument, the well, the fleeing man and exploding plane.

No one spoke. The images from a five-year-old child said enough.

***

Three weeks later, Sunnybrook Cottage hummed with its familiar morning rhythm. Leon arrived with Elena every day now, backpack slung over one shoulder, no longer clinging to her leg. He gravitated straight to the art corner, where Emily waited with a fresh sheet of paper and the full rainbow of crayons.

"Today we're drawing the garden," Emily announced. "The real one at Shadowbrook. With flowers and the fountain and no eating shadows."

Leon nodded, choosing green first. His lines were lighter, less frantic. The tall figure he once drew chasing cars now became a friendly tree. The oval-mouthed devourer became a smiling sun.

Theresa watched from the doorway, heart full. Mia sidled up beside her.

"The bus is here for our school kiddos. Look at Leon, though. He's really settling in," Mia said softly. "Jasmine says he even joined circle time yesterday. He sang the whole cleanup song."

Theresa smiled. "He's integrating. Really integrating. No more hiding in corners."

Leon looked up, caught her eye, and waved. A small, certain wave. Theresa waved back, then slipped into the kitchenette to finish her latest *Kid Quips* post.

The blog entry was titled *When Shadows Learn to Rest.*

She wrote about light winning, not through magic, but through truth spoken aloud, fears drawn out, named, and released. She shared stylized glimpses of Leon's journey, including the black crayon days, the protector shadows Maze Girl had invented, and finally the moment a child chose yellow over black. No names, no specifics, just hope wrapped in color.

At the bottom, she added a single photo of two small hands, one light, one darker, holding crayons over a bright garden drawing. No shadows in sight.

Comments poured in from parents sharing their own stories of helping kids reframe darkness, teachers thanking her for the reminder that sometimes the monsters are memories, not monsters at all. And that was all. The dark comments had been silenced, hopefully forever.

***

That evening, the house smelled of rosemary and roasted chicken. Cooking, she'd learned, was one of Alex's ways of marking small victories. A love language she could wholly get behind. Emily and Leon sat at the table, trading crayons while they waited for dinner. Elena would be arriving soon, hopefully with a folder full of properties for them to look through.

Theresa set out plates, then paused to look at the calendar on the fridge. A red circle glowed around tomorrow's date.

"Tomorrow is our anniversary," she said quietly.

Alex came up behind her, arms slipping around her waist. "What do you mean? Our wedding was festooned with wildflowers, not summertime leaves."

"Three years since you first came to the daycare for reading time." She leaned back into him. "Feels longer. And shorter, all at once."

He kissed her temple. "I love celebrating anything with you. You know, we've built a family in the middle of a storm. That's worth celebrating too."

Emily bounced over, Leon trailing behind. "Then can we have cake tomorrow? With extra sprinkles?"

"And protector candles," Leon added solemnly. "To keep the light on forever."

134

Theresa laughed, pulling both children close. "Cake, sprinkles, candles—we can have the works. And maybe a story about how shadows can become friends when you shine enough light on them."

"To new chapters," Alex said, raising an imaginary glass. "And to the ones who help us write them."

Outside, Willow Creek settled into dusk. Shadowbrook Manor stood quiet on the town's edge, no lights in the windows, no watchers beneath the trees. The well was sealed, the hidden rooms emptied, the house now waiting, not for secrets anymore, but perhaps someday for laughter, for children who would run its halls without fear.

Elena arrived, and inside their home, five plates clinked. Two children giggled over a shared crayon.

And the rainbow door at Sunnybrook waited for morning, promising another day of light, crayons, and stories that ended with everyone safe.

Theresa looked around the table at her husband, her foster-turned-forever daughter, a mother-turned-friend, and the boy who'd carried shadows too long, feeling the last tight knot in her chest loosen.

The storm was over.

The light had won.

***

"I like the one over on Clark Street. It's got a huge back room." Theresa slowly flipped through the printouts Elena had brought over. "There's a second story with an apartment setup. Might make a good tourist rental. Did you see the tiny balcony on that upstairs bedroom? It's so cute."

"I did. But look at this one." Alex tossed another sheet of paper on top of the one she'd been looking at. "There's an elevator with warehouse space on the main and second floors. That would lend itself to building a robust themed inventory. You know, keep the staples on the shelves all the time, but at Halloween, or Christmas, or Martin Luther King Day, bring out the specialty topics. I know it has a bigger retail space than we talked about, but the price is in our budget. We'd stay inside city limits, which means we'd have garbage and water from the city. And it's walking distance to Maple Café and our house. That's gotta be a sign, baby."

Theresa laughed. "I notice Maple Café took first billing there, mister."

"I go where the coffee is, what can I say." He grinned at her.

She pulled the sheet closer. "Alex, there's a rainbow."

"What?" He leaned over her shoulder. "Oh," he breathed softly. "I didn't even see that." Alex pressed a kiss against her cheek. "I'll call Elena tomorrow."

"Tell her we want to look at both properties, just in case the other one has a rainbow too."

Theresa stared up at her husband, his broad smile still sparking love in her chest. "I love you."

He swooped down and captured her lips in a soft kiss. "I love you too."

***

Theresa settled into their sunroom, the late-afternoon light casting a golden hue over her laptop screen. The room had become her sanctuary, turned into a cozy nook with overstuffed cushions, shelves of Emily's art supplies, and a window overlooking the backyard where the leaves were just starting to turn autumnal shades. Alex was in the kitchen, humming as he prepped dinner, but she'd stolen this quiet moment to draft the latest *Kid Quips* post. The blog had grown beyond her wildest dreams, now funding scholarships and playground upgrades, but it was the heartfelt comments from parents that kept her going.

She titled the draft *Shadows That Protect* and began typing, her fingers flying over the keys as the words flowed.

"Hey Quipsters,

We've all got shadows, right? Those quiet corners where worries hide. But what if we turned them into guardians? At Sunnybrook, one little artist showed us how.

Today's quip comes from our newest friend, who says, 'Shadows aren't scary if you give them a job. Like watching the swings so no one falls.'

It's a reminder that even the dark can be kind when we shine a light on it. Thank you for every tip, every share. You're helping us build brighter tomorrows.

—Miss T (and the Sunnybrook crew)"

Theresa leaned back, rereading it with a soft smile. Leon's journey had inspired it, his drawings evolving from lurking fears to golden protectors. She hit Save and called out, "Alex? Come listen to this draft. I need your bookish feedback."

He appeared in the doorway, wiping his hands on a dish towel, his eyes crinkling with that familiar warmth. "Bookish feedback? I'm your man." He perched on the arm of her chair, wrapping an arm around her shoulders. "Read away, Miss Blogger Extraordinaire."

She recited the post aloud, her voice steady but laced with emotion. When she finished, Alex kissed her temple. "Beautiful. It's got heart, like always. Makes me think of Emily's first protector drawing. It wasn't a shadow, more from her 'age of elves' days, but she drew it right after we moved in here, remember? Said it would guard the new house from 'old monsters.'"

Theresa nodded, a wave of nostalgia washing over her. Her mind drifted back to quick flashes of daycare moments that had shaped the blog, and their family.

There was Priya Delgado, perched on the circle-time rug, declaring with six-year-old wisdom, "Rainbows are bridges for feelings. They carry happy from your heart to the sky." Theresa had jotted it down mid-snack, the kids' apple slices forgotten in the magic of the moment. That quip had gone viral, funding planning to expand the sensory maze.

Then Milo, during a glitter frenzy, yelling, "My lungs are sparkly now! Rawr, disco dino!" Mia had snorted so hard she'd dropped the glue, turning cleanup into a dance party.

And Emily, whispering during naptime, "Momma T, the stars on the ceiling chase away shadow monsters. They're like hugs from the sky." That one had been the first post after the wedding, a quiet celebration of their new beginning.

The memories blurred into a montage of laughter and light, each quip a thread in the tapestry of healing they'd woven since last year's chaos.

Alex's voice pulled her back. "You're miles away. Good miles?"

"The best," she said, closing the laptop. "Just thinking how far we've come. From anonymous notes and hidden dangers to…this. Protector shadows and fundraisers."

He squeezed her shoulder. "Speaking of fundraisers, Mia texted. Seems she's knee-deep in bake sale prep and wants to know if we can swing by for taste-testing."

Theresa glanced at her phone, a new message popping up: *Kitchen apocalypse in progress. Milo thinks frosting is war paint. Save me?*

She laughed. "Let's go. Can't let her face the glitter brigade alone. Let me just see if Em wants to come along."

Their trio arrived at Mia's cozy home just as the sun dipped lower, the scent of vanilla and chocolate greeting them at the door. Mia answered, her dark hair dusted with flour, a streak of blue frosting on her cheek. "Reinforcements! Thank God. Javi's out fixing some allegedly wobbly fence at the cottage, so it's just me and the tiny terrorist."

Inside the kitchen, chaos reigned supreme. Bowls overflowed with batter, counters were a battlefield of sprinkles and cookie cutters, and Milo stood on a step stool, his face smeared with chocolate. "Miss T! Unka Alex! We're making rainbow cupcakes! But the red frosting exploded like a volcano!"

Theresa scooped him up for a hug, careful not to smudge her sundress. "Sounds epic, buddy. Did you save the day?"

Milo nodded solemnly. "I ate the evidence. Rawr!"

Mia groaned, but her eyes sparkled with amusement. "This kid. He's 'helping' by tasting everything. We need a dozen more batches for the bake sale—lemon bars, brownies, you name it. Proceeds for Leon's fund, so no pressure."

Alex rolled up his sleeves. "I'm on brownie duty. Theresa, you handle the sprinkles. I have it on good authority that your glitter expertise is unmatched."

The next hour dissolved into messy, joyful pandemonium. Mia and Theresa mixed batter while Alex and Emily entertained Milo with a dramatic reading of a recipe book, complete with voices for the ingredients— "Oh no, Mr. Flour, don't clump on me!"—while frosting flew and laughter echoed. By the end, the counters were lined with trays of treats. There were rainbow cupcakes topped with edible glitter and chocolate chip cookies shaped like protector shadows—Emily's idea.

As they cleaned up, Mia wiped her hands, grinning. "You know, this fundraiser? It's more than money. It's Willow Creek saying, 'We've got your back.' Leon deserves that."

Theresa nodded, her heart full. "And we've got each other's. Shadows or not."

Milo, sugar-high and sticky, tugged at Emily's apron. "Emmy, can shadows eat cupcakes?"

"Only the friendly ones," she replied, ruffling his curls.

As they packed boxes for the fundraiser at the community center, the evening light faded, but the warmth in the kitchen lingered. It was a tangible promise that no matter what secrets Shadowbrook still held, their light would always shine brighter.

Chapter Fifteen

Emily was pushing Leon on the Exit Express, all shadows banished to make room for story-time fun. The late-afternoon sun poured gold across the lawn, turning the rainbow door into a prism of light. Leon's laughter rang clear and unhesitant as Emily gave him another gentle push.

"Higher!" he called, legs pumping.

Emily obliged, small hands steady on the chains.

Theresa watched from the picnic table, a glass of iced tea sweating in her hand, Elena beside her. There was no tension in Elena's shoulders today, no glancing over her shoulder or shadowed eyes.

"He's different," she said quietly. "Not just the drawings. Him."

Theresa nodded. "He's letting the colors back in."

"Taking him to Dr. Macy has helped so much." Elena gently bumped against Theresa's shoulder. "Thank you for everything."

"Worth every worry to bring Leon back to himself." She paused and bumped Elena in return. "And you too."

Inside the cottage, one of Leon's latest pieces graced the art wall like a sunrise. Gone were the black-heavy colored pages; his favorites to use now were yellows, greens, and blues. The drawing showed Sunnybrook itself with the rainbow door wide open, children spilling out laughing, a single golden protector shadow standing sentinel at the fence, smiling.

Before school pickup that morning, Leon had even volunteered to share. He held up a drawing he'd done of the Shadowbrook garden showing bright flowers and a flowing fountain, then said simply, "This is where the shadows went to sleep. They're tired now."

The other children had clapped. Emily had beamed like she'd personally invented sunshine.

***

The next day, the community center was host to the fundraiser. It was a bake sale and raffle, with music by a local band, and all proceeds going to "Leon's Future Fund." Word had spread quietly through Willow Creek, everyone agreeing that the boy who'd carried the town's oldest shadows deserved a brighter path. Checks arrived from unexpected places—parents whose children attended Sunnybrook, the library staff Alex worked with, even Officer Daniels, who donated a crisp hundred with a gruff "For college. Or art school. Whatever he wants." Claire Pike had also dropped off a check earlier, waving off any thanks as she always did.

By evening, the total was enough for a modest scholarship trust. Elena accepted the envelope with tears she didn't bother hiding. "He'll have choices," she whispered to Theresa as they hugged. "Real ones."

Leon, oblivious to the grown-up weight of it all, sat cross-legged on the grass outside with Emily, drawing fireflies on dark construction paper. They were tiny glowing dots connected by golden lines. "They light up the dark," he explained when Theresa asked. "So nobody's scared anymore."

***

That night, the house glowed with string lights Alex had strung across the living room ceiling. "Anniversary leftovers," he called them. Emily sprawled on the rug, drawing with colored pencils, while Theresa and Alex curled on the couch.

Theresa scrolled idly through *Kid Quips* comments on her phone. The *Shadows Learn to Rest* post had gone quietly viral in parenting circles with thousands of shares, plus messages from therapists asking for permission to use the drawings in sessions. The tips would fund upkeep of the sensory maze for years to come.

She set the phone down and leaned into Alex. "We did it," she murmured. "We really did."

He kissed her forehead. "We started it. The kids finished it."

Emily looked up from her drawing of a new protector shadow wearing a graduation cap. "Momma

T? When Leon's big, can he come back and be a teacher here? Like you? He could teach drawing. And how to make shadows be friends."

Theresa's throat tightened. "I'd like that very much."

***

Later, after Emily was asleep, Theresa stepped over to the window for a breath of fresh air. The night was warm, stars shining sharp overhead.

Alex joined her, handing over a fresh mug of chamomile. They stood in comfortable silence for a long minute.

Then Theresa tilted her head. "You know...there's still one loose thread."

Alex raised an eyebrow.

She pointed toward the distant edge of town, where Shadowbrook's turrets were just visible against the moonlit sky. "The well's sealed. The room's empty. But Clara's diary mentioned that 'the house remembers things.' What if there's one more secret buried there? Something even Ray Hale didn't know?"

Alex followed her gaze. "You think there's another chapter?"

Theresa smiled, small, thoughtful, maybe even a little mischievous. "I think houses like that don't give up their stories so easily. And I think...maybe next summer, when Leon's ready, we'll go back. With flashlights. And crayons. And Emily. And see what else wants to come into the light."

Alex slipped an arm around her. "Together?"

"Always."

Inside, their small artist dreamed in color.

Outside, Willow Creek slept under a peaceful sky.

And far on the horizon, Shadowbrook waited, quiet, patient, one last shadow tucked safely in its corners.

Ready, perhaps, for the next story to begin.

Chapter Sixteen

The following summer, the rainbow door swung wide, Theresa's hand on her belly, ready for whatever light, or shadow, came next.

Sunnybrook Cottage glowed under strings of fairy lights, the door propped wide to welcome the entire town. Tables groaned with potluck dishes, Mrs. Tennison's delicious lemon bars, Mia's garden-fresh bruschetta, and Alex's legendary chocolate cake. Children darted between legs, chasing fireflies that had wandered in from the lawn, while parents laughed and swapped stories about the year that had almost broken them but hadn't.

Theresa stood at the center of it all, sundress fluttering in the warm breeze, her wedding band catching the light every time she reached for a hug or passed a plate. Two years since the backyard vows, three since the first anonymous note that had unraveled some of the town's oldest secrets. Tonight was for celebration. It was Sunnybrook's tenth anniversary as a daycare, and the quiet victory of a family and a community that had chosen light over fear.

Leon and Emily ruled the garden like benevolent monarchs. Leon pushed Emily on the Exit Express swing, both of them giggling as she shouted for "one more big push!" Nearby, Javi manned the bubble station, sending iridescent orbs floating into the dusk. Elena chatted with Officer Daniels by the picnic tables, her expression animated in a way Theresa hadn't seen very often.

Alex slipped up behind Theresa, arms circling her waist. "Look at them," he murmured. "All the light we fought for."

She leaned back into him. "And it's still shining."

Inside, the art wall had been cleared for the occasion. Leon's brightest drawings hung beside Emily's protector shadows, framed like treasures. One piece, jointly created by the two children, showed the entire town under a giant golden sun, every house smiling, every shadow small and harmless. A plaque beneath it read, *To the Light That Won.*

Theresa had posted about it on *Kid Quips* that morning: "When children draw their own endings, the story changes forever." The post had already garnered thousands of likes, shares, and messages of gratitude from families across the country. And tips, lots and lots of tips, which would, as always, go toward expanding and improving the daycare's playground.

As the sun dipped lower, guests began to drift home. Elena gathered Leon for bedtime, promising a sleepover soon. Mia and Javi stayed to help clean up, laughing over leftover cake.

Theresa stepped onto the porch to catch her breath. The chimes above the rainbow door tinkled softly. She reached to straighten a string of lights—and froze.

A plain white envelope rested beneath them, tucked just out of sight. No stamp, no return address. Her name in tightly drawn block letters.

Her pulse quickened. She glanced around but could see no one watching. Carefully, she opened it and read the few words on the paper, then slipped it into her pocket.

Kid Quips had hit a milestone of 400,000 followers, with a small publishing deal for a children's book based on the "friendly shadows" series, and an invitation to speak at a national early childhood conference. The blog had become more than stories. It was a movement, proof that naming fears could shrink them.

The rainbow door might be dimmer in the darkness, but the promise stayed the same.

Whatever shadows came next, they'd meet them with crayons, flashlights, and a family that had already learned how to shine.

The End

ABOUT THE AUTHOR

Raised in the south, *Wall Street Journal* and *USA Today* bestselling author MariaLisa deMora learned about the magic of books at an early age. Every summer, she would spend hours in the local library, devouring books of every genre. Self-described as a book-a-holic, she says "I've always loved to read, but then I discovered writing, and found I adored that, too. For reading...if nothing else is available, I've been known to read the back of the cereal box."

Also by MariaLisa deMora

Alace Sweets

A dark thriller, this book is not a light read. Filled with edge-of-your-seat suspense, this intense story commands the reader's attention as it drives towards the explosive ending. Alace Sweets is a vigilante serial killer, with everything that implies and is sure to trip all your triggers. Be ready.

At seventeen, Alace Sweets turned a corner in her life, taking the wrong shortcut home from school.

Resisting the harsh knowledge her attackers will never be made to pay for their actions, Alace takes a stand. Justice must be served, and if fate's scales are out of balance, she's determined to set things right as best she can.

When the laws of men fail, the rules of Alace prevail.

5-Star Reviews for Alace Sweets

"deMora has a superb story-line and exceptional character development. All of her characters have such depth that will intrigue the reader..."

~Turning Another Page

"Hot, sweet, dark thriller."

~Beth D

"It will keep you on the edge of your seat and give you chills."

~Escape Reality Book Blog

"From the first page [deMora] pulls you into the world she has created and you do not even try to escape..."

~Little Shop of Readers Blog

"A must read for all those dark, gritty romance fans out there."

~Sweet & Spicy Reads

"You will find yourself so drawn into the story that the outside world is blocked out and your locking the doors and turning on all the lights."

~Danena F

"Don't judge me for bonding with a vigilante serial killer, she's more than what she does."

~iScream Books

"Thrilling...chilling...full of suspense, nail biting edge of your seat excitement."

~Tracey H

"Every time MariaLisa deMora picks up her pen (or opens her computer), she creates characters you want to believe in."

~Gail S

"Intriguing dark storyline, beautiful love story and nail-biting conclusion, what more could a reader ask for?"

~Manda M

"This book takes you a dark and twisted ride that is gripping..."

~Renee Entress' Blog

"This book is dark and gritty and I literally had to take a day off from reading it because it's that intense."

~My Girlfriend's Couch

"This is my favourite book so far from this author ... I recommend this book if you enjoy dark romantic thrillers."

~Cheekypee Reads and Reviews

"There's not enough stars to give this book and 5 just doesn't really do it justice!"

~DeLane C

"I couldn't put this book down from page one! Tried to stop & go to bed but couldn't sleep thinking about Alace and got up & finished the book."

~Debbie M

"MariaLisa DeMora, wordsmith that she is, made this a story of the enlightenment of a woman and finding love in a life where she has had none."

~Kat W

"Whatever deep dark trench [deMora] pulled a character like Alace from should be revisited again and often."

~Confessions of a Serial Reader

SERIES AND BOOKS

Please note that books in a series frequently feature characters from early books within that series. If series books are read out of order, readers may twig to spoilers for the other books, so going back to read the skipped titles won't have the same angsty reveals.

Sunnybrook Cozy Cottage Mysteries series:

Daycare Dangers, #1
Daycare Shadows #2
Daycare Whispers, #3

Rebel Wayfarers MC series:

Mica, #1
A Sweet & Merry Christmas, #1.5
Slate, #2
Bear, #3
Jase, #4
Gunny, #5
Mason, #6
Hoss, #7
Harddrive Holidays, #7.5
Duck, #8
Biker Chick Campout, #8.5
Watcher, #9
A Kiss to Keep You, #9.25
Gun Totin' Annie, #9.5
Secret Santa, #9.75
Bones, #10
Gunny's Pups, #10.25
Never Settle, #10.5

Not Even A Mouse, #10.75
Fury, #11
Christmas Doings, #11.25
Gypsy's Lady, #11.5
Cassie, #12
Road Runner's Ride, #12.5

Occupy Yourself band series:

Born Into Trouble, #1
Grace In Motion, #2 (TBD)
What They Say, #3 (TBD)

Neither This, Nor That MC series:

This Is the Route Of Twisted Pain, #1
Treading the Traitor's Path: Out Bad, #2
Shelter My Heart, #3
Trapped by Fate on Reckless Roads, #4
Tarnished Lies and Dead Ends, #5

Rebel Wayfarers crossover stories:

Going Down Easy
No Man's Land
In Search of Solace
Puppy Love
Steel and Swagger

Mayhan Bucklers MC series:

Most Rikki-Tik, #1
Mad Minute, #2
Pucker Factor, #3
Boocoo Dinky Dau, #4

Borderline Freaks MC series:

Service and Sacrifice, #1
More Than Enough, #2
Lack of Inbetween, #3
See You in Valhalla, #4

Alace Sweets series:

Alace Sweets, #1
Seeking Worthy Pursuits, #2
Embarrassment of Monsters, #3
All the Broken Rules, #4

With My Whole Heart series:

With My Whole Heart, #1
Bet On Us, #2

If You Could Change One Thing:
Tangled Fates Stories

There Are Limits, #1
Rules Are Rules, #2
The Gray Zone, #3

Other Books:

Outlaw Heartstrings
Sidetracked Love
Only For You
Hard Focus
Salvaged Parts
Spark of the Lock
Dirty Bitches MC: Season 3

More information available at **mldemora.com**.

www.ingramcontent.com/pod-product-compliance
Lightning Source LLC
Chambersburg PA
CBHW051520030726
47592CB00006B/2355